More Praise for
The Wisdom of Yawdy Rum

"An enthralling novel set in the heart of the French Quarter. Lane's portrayal of the inner hurricane that causes turmoil in all aspects of our lives is dead on. And the lessons he bestows in *The Wisdom of Yawdy Rum* are words to live by."

— *Twin Cities Jazz Legend, Irv Williams* —

"Wow, what a trip! The tension throughout, the promise of revelation, the jazz history, the delights of the French Quarter. I'm hooked."

— *Dr. Henry Blackburn, Professor Emeritus
Division of Epidemiology, School of Public Health
University of Minnesota* —

"*The Wisdom of Yawdy Rum* is the story of a man trying to find his way in his life who meets the right mentor at the right time and is open to learning the lessons he has to teach, even when it happens under incredibly dire circumstances."

— *Mary Logue, author of* Halfway Home —

the WISDOM of Yawdy Rum

the WISDOM of Yawdy Rum

Micheal Lane

Expert Publishing Inc.

Lyrics Permissions:

"Polka Dota and Moonbeams." Words by Johnny Burke Music by Jimmy Van Heusen © Copyright 1939 by Bourne Co. and OTHER PUBLISHERS Copyright renewed All Rights Reserved International Copyright secured. Used by Permission.

"Five Foot Two Eyes of Blue Has Anybody Seen My Gal." 1925 (Renewed) EMI FEIST CATALOG, INC., RAY HENDERSON MUSIC COMPANY and WAROCK MUSIC CORP. in the U.S.A. All Rights for the World outside the USA Controlled by EMI FEIST CATALOG INC. (Publishing) and ALFRED PUBLISHING CO., Inc. (Print) All Rights Reserved. Used by Permission.

"Walking With The King." Words and Music by GEORGE "PEE WEE" ERWIN © EMI U CATALOG INC. All Rights Controlled by EMI U CATALOG INC. (Publishing) and ALFRED PUBLISHING CO., INC. (Print) All Rights Reserved Used by Permission

ISBN 13: 978-1-931945-70-7
ISBN 10: 1-931945-70-5

Library of Congress Catalog Number: 2006938156

Printed in the United States of America

First Printing: January 2007

11 10 09 08 07   5 4 3 2 1

Andover,
Minnesota

Expert Publishing, Inc.
14314 Thrush Street NW,
Andover, MN 55304-3330
1-877-755-4966
www.expertpublishinginc.com

This book is dedicated to my dad, Elvin Victor Lane.
Throughout my life, he encouraged me to believe in myself,
think my own thoughts,
and tackle anything I thought I was big enough to do.

CONTENTS

ACKNOWLEDGMENTS

To my reader, thank you for picking this book. I believe you'll find a special message contained in these pages—a message distilled and refined that will provide timeless wisdom for insight and personal growth.

I wish to convey a sincere debt of gratitude to each of the individuals who helped me complete this book. To my wife, Sharon, for her unwavering confidence and support throughout the project, and to my children, Tauna, Taylor, and Patrick, who believed in their dad. Special thanks to the musicians who helped further my understanding of traditional jazz and to those individuals who took time to review and provide feedback on the original manuscript: Dr. Henry Blackburn, Scott Craig, Charlie DeVore, Jane Hollis, Jim Holton, Isabel Keating, David Kelsey, Taylor and April Lane, Molly Peterson, Karl Speak, Doug Spong, Charlie Title, and Tauna and Shaun Wigfield. Thanks to Bev Hirt for her warmth and friendship and in leading my wife and me in a second line dance with the Preservation Hall Jazz Band. Irv Williams, thank you for the trust and friendship, and the stories you shared to help bring Yawdy to life. I thank Resa Lambert at Preservation Hall for the contacts and e-mail connections. Debbie Guidry at Preservation Hall for the gracious tour of the hall. Thanks to my writing instructor, Mary Carroll Moore, for a clear process to follow to bring the manuscript into reality, and to the outstanding editing from Mary Logue, Lynn Strickler, and Sharron Stockhausen. To my publicist, Barbara Tabor, and to the design team at Mori's Studio, thank you all very much. And to all the people who kept me energized by their constant interest in my book and its progress, thank you.

PREFACE

There are times in our lives when an idea hits us so strong it's like a giant wave washing across our consciousness. Something so strong, we feel frozen for a moment by its impact on our thoughts: an epiphany—moment of awakening or sudden insight that leaves us feeling different, somehow forever changed. I had one of those epiphany moments while I was in New Orleans in February of 2005. Following a late evening business dinner, while walking back to my hotel in the French Quarter, I stopped under the awning of Reverend Zombie's Voodoo shop on Saint Peter Street. Directly across the street, on the sidewalk in front of Preservation Hall, a line of thirty or forty people snaked along the front of the building waiting to get in. I could hear, as well as feel, the beat of the New Orleans jazz radiating from the building. Standing there staring through the drizzle at the old structure, I suddenly felt the presence of an old jazzman, his energy, and his grace. I returned to my hotel and made a few brief notes to myself about the experience. Three nights later I awoke in the middle of the night with a name on my mind. I got up, fumbled with the light in my hotel room, found a pad of paper and a pen, and wrote down the name: Yawdy Rum.

My plan had always been to leave the corporate world at an opportune time and begin a career writing and speaking. Little did I know when I first wrote down that goal over thirty years ago that an old jazzman would lead me to writing this book. I hope you enjoy reading this story. More than that, I hope Yawdy's wisdom can allow you to discover the courage to make any change you sincerely desire for your life.

ONE

A Seatmate

"Drum on your drums, batter on your banjos,
sob on the long cool winding saxophones.
Go to it, O jazzmen."

—Carl Sandburg

I leaned forward, straining against the seatbelt trying to reach my briefcase underneath the seat in front of me. A leathered dark-skinned hand reached out and stopped the tray table from an almost certain encounter with the bridge of my nose.

"Thank you," I muttered around the pen I clinched in my teeth.

"You're welcome. It looked like you needed an extra hand."

A quick glance confirmed my rescuer was a slender older black gentleman. His short, slicked down, glossy peppered hair appeared darker than the perfectly trimmed Fu Manchu adorning his chin. He seemed to be taller than me as he leaned back against the seat. He sat with crossed arms while his chest rose and fell with a deep, even breathing. I noticed his cologne earlier in the flight—mild, fragrant, snappy for an old man. He wore a glistening black nylon shirt and black slacks. A small logo affixed on the upper right front of his shirt said something about New Orleans. His shoes glistened with a fresh coat of polish. A grey tweed sport coat lay neatly folded in his lap. He pursed his lips as though he was either used to smoking a pipe or his tongue was fighting to remove some of the residual from the peanuts the airlines so graciously served us for dinner.

Until now, I hadn't paid any attention to my seatmate. Ignoring others was a habit I developed over the years to make airplane time as productive as possible. Grab your seat, store your carry-on luggage, and keep chatting to a minimum lest you'd be doomed to a conversation robbing you of some of the most productive work time of the day. Oh, it wasn't about being impolite, just being quiet and not making eye contact. Keeping to myself served as a mechanism to communicate to anyone around I was a businessperson with a full agenda. The two-and-a-half-hour late-day flight provided the opportunity to reduce my to-do list to a manageable level.

"Don't forget your book there in the seat pocket," he said.

"Oh yeah, thanks."

I let my computer slide into the center pocket of my briefcase as I turned the lock on the tray table. I pulled back the seat pocket and removed my favorite reading companion, Ralph Denyer's, *The Guitar Handbook*. I settled back in the seat and opened it to the bookmark.

You can get into your own intimate world when you sit next to the window in the coach section of a plane. It reminds me of riding in the back seat of a Volkswagen Beetle—not much room but functional enough to get the job done. The padding on the seat, the leg room, and engine rattle seem about the same. You'd think the technology required to put a modern jetliner in the air would give you some comforts to surpass those of a mid-sixties Beetle; guess again.

Trying to find enough time to develop a basic understanding of music theory required I use a few opportune moments while traveling or late at night in my hotel room. The next thirty minutes would be some of that time—woodshed time. Music theory hadn't gotten any easier to grasp because I waited until I turned fifty to try my hand at it again. I'd been at it for two years now, and the progress came painstakingly slow. I told myself I just needed to try harder this time, maybe focus and pay better attention. Paying attention was something an adult should be able to do better than a twelve- or thirteen-year-old. But no matter how hard I tried, I couldn't get my mind off my work.

I worked for an amazing variety of managers in my thirty-three years, but none as difficult as my current supervisor. In my opinion, respect is the most fundamental aspect for a successful relationship with a boss. Maybe that's what our difficulties had come to, neither of us respected the other.

"Ladies and gentlemen, this is the captain speaking. It looks like air traffic control is going to put us in a holding pattern for a bit this evening. The thunderstorm activity in the New Orleans area has traffic backed up on us. I'd like to caution you that the ride may get a bit bumpy, and suggest you make sure your seat belt is securely fastened at this time. Would the flight attendants please complete their cabin duties."

I usually found music theory to be difficult enough in smooth air; the ride tonight wasn't making it any easier.

"Studyin' a little music?" the older gentleman asked.

What an interesting voice—soft, warm, and a bit raspy, like fine sandpaper on a very light balsa wood. My eyes drifted off the page.

"Music is more of a hobby than anything. Learning it is a slow process," I said.

"It is for most folks," he replied.

"I'd rather find time to write. That's what I really like to do, but music is a great stress reliever from my work."

I boarded the plane early in Minneapolis and dug into my paperwork while the other passengers boarded. Being allowed to get on before anyone else and finding plenty of cabin space for my carry-ons offered some value for not getting an upgrade to first class. I hadn't paid any attention to those who boarded after me. I'd been engrossed in my mail and paperwork.

"What do you write about?" he asked.

"Mostly about corporate projects, presentations, narratives, and that sort of thing. I'd like to spend more time writing about practical concepts for people to use to improve the quality of their lives. Perhaps along the lines of basic truths or something similar, maybe something we already know but framed in a new and different manner, something that would enhance our lives if only we paid attention to it."

"I've found if you want to clarify somethin' that's rollin' around in your mind you have to write it out. Sort of like that music book you're holdin' onto. A composer has to take a melody that's in his mind and write down the score to make it come to life."

"Thanks, that sounds like good advice," I added.

"I couldn't help but notice the gig bag in the overhead bin. Is that yours?"

My instructor convinced me if I was ever going to learn how to play the guitar, I needed an instrument I could practice with daily on the road. A small Alvarez acoustic had become my constant companion. After all, music wasn't just about theory. I found it interesting how many people struck up a conversation out of the blue when I had it with me. They often related their own experiences about trying to develop their musical talents. Most confessed they ended the pursuit because of either the sheer difficulty or other more interesting opportunities.

"Yes, it's a guitar. I find it takes a lot of practice, so I bought one I could take on the road with me. Getting better seems to be a process of miniature steps. Do you play?"

"Yeah, but not much experience with the guitar."

"Where's home?" I asked.

"New Orleans."

"Well, it's certainly a great city for music. Of all the places I travel across the country New Orleans is one of my favorites."

"Music just seems to go with the place, been that way for a long, long time," he responded.

"I don't know much about New Orleans jazz. I hope to get a little time on this trip to enjoy a bit of it in the Quarter."

"Be careful; the Quarter can be a bit wild. This week should be relatively quiet, though. Don't think there are any major conventions in town. Are you here on business?" he asked.

"Yes."

"What kind?"

"Salt."

"Salt, you mean like table salt?"

"Yeah, like table salt," I answered.

"Somebody told me there's all kinds of salt in Louisiana. Is that true?"

"Yes, it is. Louisiana is the largest producer of mined rock salt in the country."

Maybe if I focused back on the book, the conversation could just drift back to silence. Usually when someone asked me what I did, and I mentioned salt, it turned into a game of twenty questions. Most folks couldn't understand how anyone could make a living selling salt. But it looked as if I'd satisfied his curiosity. He let his eyelids fall then relaxed back into his seat.

The tiny water droplets, streaming across the window, sparkled from the lightning flashes outside. Suddenly, the airplane dropped, only to rise again just as quickly, with the structure moaning from the stress of an early June thunderstorm that was making our evening flight as uncomfortable as possible.

The speaker overhead crackled with the voice of the flight attendant, "Ladies and gentlemen, please make sure your seat belts are securely fastened, tray tables locked and stowed, and seat backs upright. Make sure you have properly stowed any carry-on luggage you have gotten out during the flight tonight. We have been cleared into the New Orleans airport and should be on the ground shortly."

"Chord progressions can be enough of a challenge. Turbulence just adds to the attempt to sort them out," he commented.

So, the old guy was looking over my shoulder.

"Yeah, some things are better sorted out sitting in a chair on the ground."

"Well, readin' about music is one thing; feelin' it another," he offered.

I couldn't tell exactly how old he was; I'd assumed early to mid seventies. It was the tone of his voice that remained in my ear and sounded much younger than he appeared to be. I closed the music book for the evening and leaned back into my seat. My mind drifted back through the day's events. My boss and I exchanged words earlier that morning. We hadn't been getting along very well lately. We came from two complete opposites, and it seemed no matter how hard I tried, I just couldn't please him. Maybe the time approached for me to do what I wanted to in life. The corporate gig was getting old.

"You think he can land in this weather, or are we gonna have some more fun on the ride up here tonight?" my seatmate asked as one eye opened.

"My bladder is praying he'll land."

The approach wasn't as rough as I thought it might be, and it looked as if we would be off the plane by 8:30 p.m. All I had to do was grab my bag from the luggage carousel and hit National's Emerald Isle to pick up my rental car. That was the one bad thing about traveling with a musical instrument—travel restrictions instituted because of 9/11 limited carry-on bags. Bringing the guitar as my carry-on forced me to have to check a bag the last couple of years. I lost count of how much time I'd spent waiting for luggage since the government put the restrictions in place.

The aircraft door opened to allow the Gulf Coast humidity to board the plane prior to our exit. Flight attendants worked frantically to minimize the mess the turbulence created in the bathroom directly behind us. Humid air magnified the bubble gum odor of the sanitizer from the bathroom.

The older gentleman lowered his head to keep from hitting it on the overhead bin as he arose from his seat. He gave a quick wink with his right eye as he looked down at me still sitting against the window.

"Enjoy your time in New Orleans; lots of good food here in addition to the music."

"Yeah, thanks."

"Good luck with the chords."

I pulled my briefcase out from under the seat, grabbed the Alvarez from the overhead bin, and headed off the plane. The tiny green light on the face of my cell phone flashed on and off indicating a missed message. Annual purchase agreement negotiations underway with one of our largest national accounts had stalled when the buyers rejected our initial offer. More than likely our account management team completed the strategy session on our revised offer and wanted some feedback before going back to the negotiations table with the customer tomorrow morning.

I returned all of my calls by the time I stepped off the escalator in the baggage claim area. I figured if I was one of the last ones down there I'd avoid the crowd, pick up my bag, and hit the door. The empty baggage carousel, its black rubber belt making a constant squeaking sound at each turn, snaked through the waiting area. It looked as if several minutes passed since anything resembling a suitcase had come off the belt. The older fellow who had been my seatmate stood across the carousel from me. The only other passenger from our flight was a bored looking younger female sitting on the floor at the end of the carousel apparently waiting on her luggage as well. I made eye contact with my old seatmate.

"You may have to wait a bit before you get any time for pickin' on that guitar," he said.

"Yeah, it doesn't look like we're going to have any luck here. I've been on my phone upstairs. I figured all the bags would be in by now. Fifteen minutes is my limit. Let's see what Northwest has to say."

We made our way around a sea of black suitcases and bags to the doorway of the Northwest baggage claim office. It was recessed behind a glass panel in between the two carousels. A line of three or four tired looking passengers stood waiting at the counter. We heard the agent say there had been a weight problem in Minneapolis with extra fuel being required because of weather, so we must have been the lucky ones and had our bags left behind.

In no time we were at the counter, my seatmate standing in front of me. After a few minutes of his fingers racing across the computer keyboard, the agent looked up and said, "Uh, well, uh, it looks like ya'lls bags will be here on the 10:15 p.m. flight. And, uh, it looks like it's gonna to be a little late tonight as well. If you'll give us the name of your hotel, we'll have your bags forwarded, Mr. Rum."

"No, that's fine," he said. "I live at 2113 Chartres in Marigny."

Marigny, that sounded familiar. I wonder how long he'd....

"Were you also on the flight from Minneapolis?" The agent asked as I took my place at the counter.

"Yes." I handed him my baggage claim ticket, lowered the Alvarez in its soft-sided bag to the floor, and opened my briefcase to get my planner. "Let me take a look at my planner for the name of my hotel. I think I'm at the Hotel Saint Marie on Toulouse Street in the Quarter."

He waited with his hands on the yellowed keyboard of his computer terminal while I confirmed the name of my hotel. "That'll be no problem. We'll have your bags put on a taxi and delivered to the hotel later tonight," the agent said in a most confident manner.

I looked at my fellow traveler still standing next to me in line at the counter. "I've got a rental car, and I'm going to the Quarter. I'm happy to give you a ride if Marigny is anywhere near there."

He put out his hand and said, "Sure, and the name's Rum, Yawdy Rum. Yours?"

"Micheal Lane, but I go by Mike. Sorry I didn't introduce myself sooner."

"That's okay. I appreciate the ride."

"Great! Besides, I have a connection to the Marigny district," I added.

TWO

The Claudet Connection

*"Folk songs: These are the treasure of lovely melodies
and will teach you the characteristics of nations."*

—Robert Schumann

"All songs are folk songs."

—Louis Armstrong

A thud came from the rear tire as it dropped off the curb from me cutting the corner a bit short as we pulled into the Taco Bell off Airline Highway.

"You okay with drive thru?" I asked.

"Fine by me. All I need is a little somethin' to drink."

"I've never been able to get enough Mexican food. And when you're on the road, it's tough to eat right. I figure rice and beans have to be better for you than a burger and fries, especially this late at night. What is it—almost 10:00 p.m.?"

"My watch says it's a bit after. Some folks down here exist almost entirely on red beans and rice," he offered.

"I don't think Taco Bell has made the jump to red beans yet, maybe one of these days."

"Mr. Rum, what can I order for you?"

"Small Pepsi be all I need."

The turquoise plastic frame around the drive-up speaker rattled along with a voice that was nearly impossible to understand. In addition to what sounded like a mouthful of yellow-blue cat's-eye marbles, the clerk's Cajun accent made understanding the repetition of our simple order an impossibility.

"You sell these guys salt?" Yawdy asked. "I guess, that is, if you are in the sales end of things."

"Actually, I'm the director of sales and marketing, but I try to stay involved with what we do on an account level. Taco Bell is a part of Yum Brands along with Colonel Sanders and Pizza Hut."

"Hmm, somethin' for ol' Rum's tum from the folks at Yum. Always in sales?"

"No, my wife likes to say I started below ground and worked my way up, been in the business over thirty years. I worked at a salt mine in Kansas when I was going to college."

"I didn't know there were salt mines in Kansas. Didn't you tell me on the plane that Louisiana had an edge on salt mines?"

"Louisiana has some of the best rock salt in the country, but there are mines in other places as well."

"What's it like workin' in a salt mine?" he asked.

"Not bad at all. Most mines maintain a constant temperature in the seventies year around. No bad dust like a coal mine and a heck of a lot safer, too."

"How deep you guys go to mine salt?"

"Over at Avery Island we mine at about sixteen hundred feet."

Yawdy's eyes opened and the furrows deepened on his forehead, "Ooo eeee, that would be too far from the grass for this ol' boy."

Giant raindrops spattered the windshield as we pulled out onto I-10. I was trying to drive with my knee and get the hot sauce in the cup of beans without getting it all over me, when Yawdy reached over and steadied the wheel with his left hand.

"Here, let me help you out," he offered.

"Thanks. That's twice tonight you've given me a hand. I appreciate it. You'll have to tell me where to drop you off. I didn't catch your address in Marigny."

"Just stay on I-10, hop off at 236, then over to Esplanade. It's only about ten blocks south from there. I appreciate the ride. It's been a long day."

"Don't some folks call the Marigny district by another name?" I asked.

"Some call it the lower French Quarter."

"Where did the name Marigny come from?"

"Marigny was a plantation here at the time of the Louisiana Purchase. Guess the name just stuck."

I took a spoonful of the beans and continued, "I mentioned I have a connection to Marigny. I had a great-aunt and uncle who lived in the Quarter. I met them a couple of times when I was growing up in Kansas, but never did get down here just to see them before they both passed away. I used to call my great-aunt on the phone when I came through here earlier in my career, but there never seemed to be enough time to get to her place. I think when I was younger, I felt everything had to be in a rush. Too bad we don't learn to slow down a bit until we get older."

"Largo," he responded. "It's a musical term, means to slow down. It's somethin' we all need to be aware of. What was your aunt's name?"

"Goldie. Goldie Claudet. Her husband's name was…."

"Amos," Yawdy interrupted.

"Yeah, how'd you know that?"

"Well, if your great-aunt was the Goldie Claudet who played the piano some at Pat O'Brien's, her husband's name was Amos."

"I didn't know she played the piano on a professional basis."

"The duelin' pianos at O'Brien's are more about good old-fashioned New Orleans fun than about professional music. But let me tell you, did she ever know how to make those ivories sing."

We had traveled several blocks toward the river on Esplanade when he said, "You can just let me off down here at the corner at Chartres if you'd like. You can turn right on Decatur to get over to your hotel. Didn't I hear you tell the baggage guy you were stayin' at the Saint Marie?"

"Sure am, but didn't *you* tell *me* that a person needs to keep an eye out for themselves in the Quarter?"

"Yeah, I guess I did."

"I'll be glad to drop you off at your place."

"Okay. I'm just about a block up Chartres at 2113 on the left."

We pulled over to the curb along the narrow street as a steady rain continued to fall. The wipers displayed an intermittent hesitation as they streaked across the windshield. I looked across the street to an older white duplex. Tall emerald green doors stood on each end of the front porch with identical green framed windows centered on the front of the house behind the wooden porch railing. Old shimmering brass coach lamps affixed next to each door lit velvet red steps up to each end of the duplex.

"Did you know my great-aunt?" I inquired.

"Yes, I did. But I probably knew Amos a little better than Miz Goldie."

"I knew they lived somewhere in the Marigny district," I added.

"They lived just up the street on the other side of Elysian Fields. I know the house, but don't 'member the number. Amos died a long time ago, but I think Miz Goldie stayed in the house up 'til she took ill and passed on ten or fifteen years after he did."

When he spoke, his eyes squinted a bit, and a wide smile framed his face. It was hard to tell how old he was, but this man was no youngster. There was something about him, a sense of calm, and warmth that made me feel I had known him all my life.

"I'd like to know a bit more about them sometime if you have a few minutes."

"Sure, I suppose we could do that."

"Were you in Twin Cities or just connecting through on your way home?" I asked.

"I was in the Twin Cities."

"Business or pleasure?"

"This week it's been a little of both. The Hall has a concert booked in Minneapolis, and I was there bein' interviewed for a commercial they are makin', and visitin' an old friend of mine."

"The Hall?" I asked.

"Yeah, an old jazz place here in the Quarter."

"What's the name of the band?"

"The Preservation Hall Jazz Band. Some say it's a bunch of old musicians workin' to keep New Orleans jazz alive, but it's really New Orleans jazz musicians tryin' to keep themselves alive. I'd be glad to talk to you some more when I'm a bit fresher. It's gettin' late, and I've got a full day tomorrow. I sure thank you for the ride tonight. I hope your luggage shows up at the hotel."

He pulled open his tweed sports coat and reached into the inside pocket. He handed me a small blue piece of paper.

"If you've got some free time this week, you might enjoy this. I should be there most of the week. If you'd like to chat a bit more about your family, stop by and see me."

We shook hands, Yawdy opened his door and stepped out. He walked around the front of the car and headed up the sidewalk to the waiting red steps on the left side of the duplex, his black leather handbag slung over his shoulder. As I pulled away from the curb, I again wondered how old he was. Was he married? Did he have a family? He knew my Great-aunt Goldie. How about that! I unfolded the blue note he handed me. It was a ticket. It read, "Admit One, Preservation Hall, 726 Saint Peter Street, New Orleans, Louisiana."

THREE

The Saint Marie

"Our sweetest songs are those which tell of saddest thought."

—Percy Shelley

The white lace curtains billowed out of the open French doors on the second floor balcony as I pulled up in front of the Saint Marie and parked along the curb. I glanced at my watch. It was almost 11:00 p.m. The soft glow from inside made the curtains appear as though the spirit of the hotel was escaping on the evening breeze to Bourbon Street. A smart looking little doorman, dressed in a royal blue uniform with shiny brass buttons and a crisp matching cap with a violet brim, stepped around from behind the rear of the car as I got out.

"How we be doin' dis evenin'?" he asked.

"Just fine. And you?"

"If'n I was any better, I cudn't stand it. You be stayin' at da Saint Marie?"

"All week," I answered.

He handed me a valet parking ticket, and said, "Let me hep you wit yo bags, and w'lcome to da Quarter."

"No need for that. Northwest decided my bag would be better off on a later flight."

"Well, we gots a special kit for folks just like you dat looses da bags. Ya'll be sure and ax Miss Eloise on da desk, and she be takin' care of you."

I grabbed my briefcase and the light tan gig bag with the Alvarez out of the back seat and handed the car keys to the doorman. His eyes opened a bit wider when he noticed the instrument case.

"You be playin' in da Quarter?"

"Oh, no, just a traveling companion."

"Well, sir, ya'll be havin' a good time while you's wit us."

"I'll do that. Thanks."

I'd found the Saint Marie on one of my earlier trips to New Orleans. It was a lovely eighteenth century style hotel, located just off Bourbon Street, in the heart of the French Quarter. Crisply painted black ironwork framed the second story balcony and sidewalk canopy. The beat of New Orleans jazz from the bars on Bourbon Street filtered through the humid night air and caught my attention as I reached for the front door of the hotel. *No, not this late,* I thought. *Better finish off the e-mail and give Sharon a quick call at home to let her know I made it.*

"Good evening, and welcome to the Saint Marie," the desk clerk remarked. "Will you be checking in?"

"You should have a reservation for Lane. First name's Mike."

The white marble floor of the lobby shined to perfection. A gardener, in a crisp green uniform, working in the center of the lobby, snipped away at a vase of color from exploding translucent orchids, blue delphinium, curly willow, yellow sunflowers, and hot pink roses. A chandelier hanging above the table danced with the reflection of the rainbow of colors from the flowers below. The clerk confirmed the room and handed me a folder with the room keys.

"Your room is on the second floor, Mr. Lane. The elevator is behind you, across the lobby. Will you need any help with your bags, sir?"

"Just getting my roller bag. The Northwest agent said it should be here later tonight. Could you see that it is delivered to my room when it arrives?"

"Sure thing. Did they give you a time?"

"Nope, just sometime before morning."

"One more thing, Mr. Lane. Maintenance is working on our boiler, and we are currently without hot water. We hope that won't be too much of an inconvenience for you."

"No more than I've already been through tonight. Will it be fixed by morning?"

"Yes, sir, we believe so."

Somehow I felt it was going to be a cold shower in the morning. The elevator door rattled as it opened to the second floor, and I stepped out onto the shimmering white marble tile. I turned left down the hallway and found room 244. I slipped the key card into the slot, and the light on the lock sparkled green as I rotated the handle. I leaned against the weight of the door as I stepped in the room. There was just something about a nice hotel—fresh smelling rooms, clean carpet, dark rich walnut furniture, and bright colors. I didn't really care if Motel 6 left the light on. I'd take the Saint Marie any day.

I stood the Alvarez securely against the end of the credenza with my briefcase next to it, and I sprawled across the bed. The air whished out of the fluffy pillow at the headboard as I leaned back into it, cradled the phone against my shoulder, and dialed home. I never knew how long a call home would take. My wife, Sharon, a master at holding things together when I was gone, almost always waited up for my phone call at the end of a day. I called to let her know I'd made it safely to my hotel, and to check in on the latest developments at home. Our two older children had always been like delayed twins, Tauna, twenty-six, lived downtown Minneapolis, and her brother Taylor, fifteen months younger, lived in Tampa, Florida. They still seemed to look to their mom for help with an assortment of things–listening to their newest challenge, sharing news in their lives, being a safe sounding board, and simply staying connected. Our youngest, Patrick, a nineteen-year-old autistic boy, was still living at home with us. Sharon was always saying it was no wonder her hair turned prematurely gray, with her carrying so much of the load on the home front. As a stay-at-home mom, she held things together in my absence. I felt bad when things were in chaos at home and I was gone. It was a helpless feeling with which I had never come to terms, but we each understood our roles in raising and providing for our three kids.

"Well, my day started off in one direction and abruptly changed course. Taylor said his roommate is moving back to Minnesota. I guess he just didn't like Florida."

"And now I suppose Taylor's got a problem covering the lease and needs a little help."

"No, he just wanted us to know."

"What was up with Tauna?" I asked.

"Tauna's car quit, so I had to pick her up and get her from the apartment to work in Corcoran. I drove about a hundred miles today for that girl."

"And did she tell you *thanks?*"

"Oh, yeah, right. I'm just a fixture around here. I think if I dyed my hair green, got a few tattoos, and bought a Harley, I might get a little attention for myself."

"How about Patrick, how did his day go?"

"He came home in a foul mood, and we almost never got through the work from the tutor. No wonder I'm graying, taking all the crap from that boy. And, get this, they are going to have the road torn up for some type of sewer repairs for the next few days. We are having to park across the road in the church parking lot. Want to hear more?"

As usual, I mostly listened. It helped us to stay connected. It helped us to be a team even though I was gone. Being a thousand miles from home, what could I do except give her my support? The past few years, the travel had been more intense than ever. I was growing tired of always being gone and never being at home for more than a few days at a time. Deep down inside, my goal was to find a way out of the corporate rat race. I wanted to bid farewell to the demands of corporate politics. I wanted to write and develop a professional speaking business. It wasn't the long hours—I never minded working hard; I wanted the opportunity to set my own schedule—to work for myself. "You mean there is more?"

"I know, I know, I'm just venting. How about you? Did you get to New Orleans okay?"

"Yeah, sort of, although Northwest didn't get my bag on the flight."

"Since you started traveling with that guitar you've certainly had more than your share of baggage problems."

"The baggage agent said, it's supposed to come in on the next flight. I'm hoping it gets here before morning."

"Can you hold on for just a minute?" she asked.

In the background, I could hear her holler at Patrick to get out of the shower. Autism was proving to be just as difficult to understand and deal with, now that he was a teenager, as it had been when he was younger. Transitions from one activity to another, nothing special for most of us, can be earth-shattering events for an autistic person. For Patrick, simply getting in or out of the shower could develop into a major event.

"Mike, I have to go. I just heard a crash upstairs. I hope your luggage arrives. Talk to you tomorrow night?"

"We've got meetings all day, and a dinner that I know will go late, and I've got this ticket. It's to... Hello, Sharon, Sharon?..."

FOUR

A Run in the Quarter

"If it ain't got swing, it ain't worth playin'."

—Bubber Miley

Prior to my trip to New Orleans, I arranged to meet Grantland Robique, our southern regional sales manager, for a run in the French Quarter. The week prior, Grantland sent an e-mail confirming he would also be staying at the Saint Marie. We were both in town for the quarterly review meeting.

I could always count on Grantland to show up for an early morning run. He loves putting it on me. Although, he is several years older than I am, he still has the stride of a yearling thoroughbred. I enjoy talking with him on our runs, if I can keep my breath. He's been in the salt business longer than me, and I value his perspective on things.

A muscled figure in blue shorts, and a well-worn white T-shirt was warming up just inside the front door of the lobby when I stepped off the elevator. Stretching his two-hundred-pound frame, Grantland didn't notice me walk up behind him.

"Hey, ol' man, ready for a run?" I asked.

"Morning. I was beginning to wonder if you made it in okay."

"Yeah, but my bag didn't make it on my plane so the airline put it on a later flight. I didn't get it until about four this morning. I was thinking I would have to pass on you if I didn't get my running shoes. How was the drive over from Lafayette?"

"It was fine. Actually, I drove through Avery Island on my way over yesterday. I picked some stuff up at the mine for our meeting this week."

"Where do you want to run this morning?" I asked.

"It stopped raining, so let's head over front o' town and down river along Peters. How far are you up for?"

I clicked the timer on my watch. "Looks like we've got time for four, or maybe five, miles. Are you going to tie those shoes?"

"No, you know me. I've got to give you some kind of handicap, and I don't want to leave you too far behind."

"Aren't you nice," I added.

We stepped over a bulging rust-colored water hose snaked out through the double French doors of the Saint Marie. It seemed to be waiting for someone to begin the early morning sidewalk wash. Our breathing began to increase along with the quickening pace as we jogged the first couple of blocks towards riverside on Toulouse. The air hung heavy in the Quarter with a mixture of the stench of libations that had been spilled along the street the night before and the unmistakable background odor of urine.

"Nothing like running in the Quarter to jump start the senses," I offered.

"No place like it."

"I met an interesting fellow on the plane last night."

"Oh yeah, who was that?" he asked.

"An older man who lives over on the down-river side of the Quarter and has some kind of connection with Preservation Hall."

"A musician?"

"I think so."

"Young, old?" Grantland asked.

"I'm guessing he's in his seventies, trim, and was dressed pretty sharp. He has a snowy white Fu Manchu. Man, is it striking on his black face. His bags got left in Minnesota with mine, so besides sitting together on the plane, we were both waiting at baggage claim at the same time last night."

"I thought you didn't talk on airplanes."

"Well, not usually, but he noticed my guitar book and struck up a conversation."

"Are you making any progress on your picking?"

"Maybe, a little, but it's slow. Just finding any extra time is the hard part. I think the salt business would consume every minute of my time if I'd let it. You know my favorite saying: This company won't kill you, but they'll let you kill yourself."

I could hear him chuckle over my accelerated breathing as we turned down river on Decatur. "Grantland, how have you dealt with it all these years? You've been here longer than I have."

"Just tried to keep my head down and get the job done."

"I'd say it's worked pretty well for you. I've never been able to do that."

"No, Mike, you talk too much. Something comes across your mind and it comes out your mouth. You see more clearly around here than anyone what it takes to make this company successful, and when the honchos take off on some wild goose chase, consuming valuable resources, you call 'em on the carpet for it. That's what keeps you in hot water."

"How much are you charging for this session, Doc?"

"Free, it's on me this morning. Come on, let's pick up the pace."

We ran along the inside of the levee on Peters at a good clip. Grantland was built like a middleweight wrestler, yet it seemed effortless for him to trek along at an eight-minute-per-mile pace.

"I'm about to die over here, and you are hardly breaking a sweat this morning," I gasped.

"It takes living down here to get used to the humidity. So what made the guy you met last night seem so interesting?"

"I gave him a ride home from the airport, and it turned out he knew some relatives of mine that used to live in the Quarter."

"Oh, yeah. Did he share any interesting stories?"

"No, we really didn't get to talk that long. It was getting late, and he wanted to get home. He gave me a ticket to get into Preservation

Hall to listen to some New Orleans jazz this week. Are you up for it one night?"

"I'll pass. I'm going to attend the dinners we've got scheduled, but I'm going to hide out after that and see some friends."

As we ran along the inside of the levee, we could see the silhouette of the stack of a tug working on the river. The heavy chugging of the diesel engine made the boat sound as if it was on top of us. The moisture in the dark morning air magnified the effect.

"Grantland, I've heard that New Orleans is something like seven or eight feet below sea level, and there are pumps that run day and night to keep the city dry. Is that true?"

"Yes, it is. I think the Army Corps of Engineers put in pumps back in the twenties or early thirties to keep the city dry. I've heard the city can cope with about an inch or two of rain an hour. Any more than that and the water starts to back up."

"What's the plan if the city gets hit by a storm and dumps more rainfall than they can handle?" I asked.

"Good question. Start paddling, I guess."

A mangy, old German shepherd followed us for several blocks after we turned towards back o' town on Polland Street. His growly bark drove a chill down my spine. The sky was just starting to lighten at the turn. The faint sunlight framed the dog's silhouette in the early morning mist. My watch confirmed it was a little before 6:15 a.m.

Grantland continued, "They say the French chose the Quarter as a place to build because it was the highest ground in the whole area. Back then, there were no levees, so they observed the spring floods and learned which ground was safe. Guess someone was paying attention. I know one thing, though…"

"Yeah, what's that?" I asked.

"I sure wouldn't want to be here in a bad storm."

The remainder of the run was quiet, just breathing, sweat, and an occasional dog bark. By the time we turned the corner back to the hotel, the city was coming to life. All sizes of city delivery trucks began unloading various sizes of boxes and containers to the purveyors in the Quarter. The sky appeared as a soft flannel, although the heaviness of the Gulf humidity hung like a veil in the steamy morning air. We walked the last three or four blocks to the hotel.

"Let's hope the hot water is working," Grantland offered.

"As warm as I am, it might be better to take a cold shower. Give me about thirty minutes and I'll meet you back downstairs."

The light on my phone was blinking when I got back to my room. After fumbling with the instructions for a few minutes, I figured out how to access the voice mail for the hotel, and picked up a message from Sharon.

"Hi, dear, I got your message. What's up?"

"Sorry I had to hang up on you last night, but you know how crazy it can be around here with Patrick getting ready for bed."

"Don't worry about hanging up on me; I understand what you're dealing with."

"Did you get a run in this morning?"

"Yeah, I met Grantland, and we did about four miles through the Quarter, and along the river. I just never get used to running in the heat and humidity down here."

"Your package came in the mail from the writing class."

"Did you open it?"

"No, it's addressed to you. Patrick wanted to, but I told him it was Dad's. How do you think you're going to find the time for a writing class when you're gone almost every week? You might have to give up the guitar if you are serious about writing."

"Yeah, I know. And I certainly don't see any breaks in my travel schedule."

"I just don't know where you can find the time to write a book."

"I'm still planning to walk away from all of this when I turn fifty-five, and that's only three years away. I don't know how to find the time before then, other than continuing to hone my writing skills so I can hit the ground running when I'm free from the salt business."

"I think we both need job changes. It gets old, being a single parent most of the time, dealing with the challenges of an autistic teenager. What am I saying? He vacillates between teenager and toddler."

"I know it's a challenge, Sharon. I don't have any short-term answers."

"I know you don't. No one does, and I'm not asking for any."

"I met an interesting fellow on the plane last night."

"Who was that?"

"An older guy, his name is Yawdy Rum."

"Rum, like the rum you drink?"

"Yeah, I think so. He has something to do with the jazz place here in New Orleans called Preservation Hall. He gave me a free ticket."

"Well, that's right up your alley. I know you like all kinds of music."

"Yeah, it sounds fun and what's more fun is he knew Great-aunt Goldie."

"No kidding. How'd he know her?" She asked.

"He really didn't say. I'm hoping he can fill in a few details. Hey, I might even learn a little about jazz."

"Dear, I'll talk to you tonight. I gotta go."

The telephone receiver dropped into the cradle with a click, and I headed for the shower.

"Damn, cold water."

FIVE

On Saint Peter Street

"Jazz? Bah–nothing but the debasement of noble brass instruments by blowing them into mutes, hats, caps, nooks, crannies, holes, and corners."

—Sir Thomas Beecham

With everything we know about a human being's ability to pay attention and remain fresh, it slays me that a company would run an all-day meeting, and then a three-hour dinner with barely a break or chance to refresh yourself.

I was beginning to have a harder and harder time with the corporate demands. Maybe because I was getting older and had done it for so long, I just didn't have the patience with it I once did. Perhaps that's what happens to us all. We work to get to a level where we think we can affect a change in how things are done, and we become even more trapped by the culture and the expectations the organization places on us. We find ourselves at a point where we'd like to pursue some of our own interests, yet the demands of the company consume our very existence. Every senior manager above me seems engulfed by their corporate position, power, and trappings.

"Sir, this evening at Chez Paul's we are serving café au lait from extra dark chicory. Would you like some?"

"Yes, I would. Thank you."

The aroma from the roasted chicory overtook all of us at the table as she poured. I stirred the coffee she placed in front of me and envisioned the spoon standing straight up in the middle of the cup. The tiny muscles in my fingers holding the spoon seemed to flex against the strain of the powerful brew. This wasn't like regular coffee; it was like a magnum load of espresso to the second power. It made my palms sweat just to hold the white porcelain cup. I'd always heard that chicory was supposed to make coffee smoother. To me, it was just the opposite, just plain bitter, but it had been a long day, a longer dinner, and a revival was in order.

Geez, was I full. I looked over at Grantland, sitting about half way down the table from me. "Which one of us is going to pop first?"

"What did you have?" he asked.

"Deep fried duck, served with a boudin butter cream sauce, fresh swordfish with roasted pecans, jalapenos, and a browned garlic butter and lemon glaze."

"Was that all?"

"Oh yeah, and sweet potato pie with this depth-charged coffee," I added.

"We're headed to the bar for a quick nightcap before we walk back to the hotel. Want to join us?"

"No, thanks. I need to walk a bit to work off some of my dinner. I'm going to see if I can take in a bit of jazz up on Bourbon Street before the night is over. Anyone interested?" I asked as I glanced up and down the table, no takers.

The wooden frame of my chair squeaked as I slid back from the table, took the last gulp of the cream-laced coffee, and stood up.

"Do you want to run in the morning? I think we have some others who may join us," Grantland asked.

"What's the weather look like?"

"Rain. You're in New Orleans."

"I'll meet you in the lobby at 5:30 a.m. unless it's raining hard."

I walked out into the street and felt a bit of relief to have some time of my own. As I slid my right hand into my pants pocket, my fingers wrapped around the ticket Yawdy gave me. My watch said it was 10:17 p.m. That's early for New Orleans, I thought as I walked along Chartres Street.

I stopped on the east side of Saint Peter at a small shop filled with a mishmash of African and Jamaican art and trinkets. A large, round, white, wooden sign, with red lettering hung above the doorway. It advertised Reverend Zombie's Voodoo Shop. I wondered if Reverend Zombie would have any insight helping bring balance into this experience called life. Maybe I could buy a voodoo doll, and take care of a few folks that were giving me fits. The earthy fragrance of patchouli wafted out the doorway onto the sidewalk. It was coming from a tarnished silver incense burner hanging just inside the store. I'd only spent a couple of minutes studying a wild array of hoops, rings, African art, and voodoo-related paraphernalia, when a clerk approached me. She was adjusting the black scarf tied around her neck, along with a plumage of classic, New Orleans gold, emerald green, and iridescent purple Mardi Gras beads. She had a small frame and jet black hair pulled back close to her scalp. She looked to be thirty, maybe younger. My index finger filtered through a black, wooden box with two-inch square compartments holding all sorts of miniature musical instruments in the form of shiny charms.

"You like the gris-gris?" she asked.

I'm sure I looked puzzled. She must have noticed, because she quickly added, "The voodoo charms, the gris-gris. They bring good luck."

"What's the voodoo connection with New Orleans? Did it get started originally with the French?" I asked.

"There was a slave uprising in the French colony of Saint Domingue in the 1700s, and a number of people from there immigrated to New Orleans. A few years later, after a Haitian revolution, many thousand refugees came to the city. They brought the practice of voodoo with them," she explained.

"Sounds like you're an expert."

"I think there may be something to voodoo. And I think you would feel better with the gris-gris in your pocket," she responded, as she repositioned the box of charms a bit closer to me.

"Thanks, I think I'll pass. Do you know where Preservation Hall is located?"

"It's right behind you, across the street," she answered. "They have very good gris-gris over there."

I turned and glanced across Saint Peter Street to a stained, stucco gray, two-story building. As soon as I focused on it, I realized a muffled mix of New Orleans jazz was emanating from inside. However, it got lost on the street with the raucous music filtering down from the bars on Bourbon Street. There was a black iron railing all along the balcony on the second floor across the front of the building. Behind it there were three sets of closed wooden hurricane doors. I didn't see a sign on the front of the building, but noticed the numbers 726 to the left of the doorway. They matched the numbers on the ticket Yawdy had given me a couple nights earlier. The entrance was at street level on the right-hand side of the building as I faced it from Reverend Zombie's.

"Thanks for your time, ma'am, maybe I'll stop back."

The wet pavement glistened as I walked across the street and up to a round shouldered gentleman standing in a line of about thirty people on the sidewalk. "Are you waiting in line to get in?" I asked.

"Yep, the end of the line is back there; it isn't moving too fast. Guess the old jazz they are playing inside is just too good to walk out on," he answered. "The guy at the door only lets in a few folks at a time. I think it's the second set. The last time I was here, they didn't close up until after 2:00 a.m."

"Thanks," I said, as I walked towards riverside on the sidewalk and took a place at the end of the line. I leaned back against the support of the wall behind me and took in the faint, stinging aroma of cigarette smoke wafting down Saint Peter. Even though I was fifteen or twenty feet from the south edge of the Preservation Hall building, I could feel the music vibrating through the wall behind me. Not strong mind you, just a light tingle that caught my attention, an energy force moving through the mortar.

By 11:00 p.m. the line moved far enough along the sidewalk for me to see through the glazed window on the front of the building. An older, short, gray-haired lady carrying a bulging paper shopping bag stood in front of me in line on the sidewalk. She spoke with a thick Brooklyn accent.

"They used the Hall for a scene in a Steve McQueen movie back in the sixties. That's when they glazed over the clear glass in the windows. Doesn't it just give it a remarkable effect?" she asked.

I agreed, as I peered into the building.

"I just love this music," she offered. "There's nothing like it."

"I'm not that familiar with Dixieland jazz. I just like music in general," I replied.

"Oh, this is different from Dixieland jazz. Honey, they're playing traditional New Orleans jazz. You can tell by listening."

I wasn't sure what I was supposed to be listening for–New Orleans or Dixieland. I'd just assumed they were one and the same. I peered into the Hall through the glazed window. Five or six musicians had their backs to the windows, facing the interior of the room, playing to an audience of maybe fifty people packed into the place. The smiling faces, handclapping, and head bobbing appeared to be a clear sign of audience engagement.

In not more than ten minutes my place in line moved to the main opening and into the breezeway leading into the building. It seemed there was a steady conversion going on in the audience, as one or two jazz revelers filtered out, and the heavyset little gentleman working the doorway let an equal number of jazz aficionados in to partake of the preservation being offered in the Hall.

As I stepped around an old wrought iron gate swung open in the doorway, the doorkeeper looked up at me. "You by yourself?" he asked.

"Yep."

"I've got a bit more room if you'd like to squeeze in." Barely taller than the cabinet behind him, he was a stocky little fellow, with a brown sweat-stained felt porkpie hat, and a well-worn gray T-shirt. A large hairy mole about twice the size of a pea grew on the bridge of his nose. The bass drum imprint on the front of the doorkeeper's T-shirt matched the shape of his belly. The words Preservation Hall Jazz Band in fading red letters encircled the drum on his shirt.

"It'll be eight bucks."

"Looks like your assistant fell asleep on you," I commented.

He turned and looked down at a lanky old white cat curled up on the frayed cushion on the chair, next to a wooden rack of Preservation Hall CDs, and T-shirts.

"That's ol' Champ's usual position. He's been awfully tired tonight. Some folks were here earlier from the *USA Today* newspaper and took his picture. I think it wore him out. If they print it, and he becomes famous, he'll give us fits."

I handed him the ticket Yawdy had given me. "Will this get me in?"

"Ah, sure, but you might want to save it for a night when you could get in earlier. You'd get a better deal that way."

"That's okay."

He motioned to the raised doorway on the left side of the carriage way leading into the same room I'd peered into from the sidewalk. The place was cooking. My body wanted to move with the music, almost like something had gotten into my knees, and made them want to rock with the beat, something at a primal level. My guitar teacher, Pete back in Minneapolis, had said more than once, "You need to feel the rhythm with your whole body, to get into music." Maybe this was what he was talking about.

I slipped around behind the people crowded in just past the door and along the back wall, until I could find an opening to see the band. There certainly wasn't an abundance of light in the place. Two conduits hung down from the ceiling and connected with square-bladed fans and frosty, fly-specked lights. They were like faintly glowing lamps suspended above the crowd and seemed to be wobbling a bit with the music. In the front row of the band, just right of center, proud as you please on an old high-back wooden dining room chair, sat Yawdy. He was squawking out a solo of an old New Orleans dance tune on a shiny black clarinet. The lady standing next to me said it was "Back Porch." His eyes were wide open, absorbing the faces in the crowd as he played. The emotion of the song reflected in the muscles of his face. The long, broad lines across his forehead almost looked like a musical staff. The instrument wasn't something apart from him; he projected himself through it. I could tell it was second nature to him.

A large pedestal fan standing behind the piano circulated in time with the music. An old upright piano with nearly all the front missing provided a frame for the right side of the band. There appeared to be only a narrow rail along the front edge to hold sheet music from falling back into the piano. The band members all wore white dress shirts and dark pants. Some had neckties, and some didn't. Those who did had all loosened the knots long before now, if they'd ever been tight at all. The exception was the piano player. She was a full-figured lady wearing a blousy pink dress with a cascade of printed red carnations down the front. It looked like every part of her was flowing with the music. She wore a webbed band of jingle bells just below her right knee that caught on the hem of her dress as her legs bounced up and down with the beat.

A trombone player on Yawdy's far right swayed back and forth in tempo. He looked to be much older than Yawdy, but his command of the instrument seemed equally polished. Waiting his turn on the trumpet, the only white gentleman in the band, sat front and center next to Yawdy. The two front windows framed the bass player standing against the back wall. Faces from those still standing in line outside on the sidewalk trying to see in were plastered to each of the windows. The bass player, a tall lanky gentleman, had bushy dark arching eyebrows that turned down almost to his cheekbones. Bouncing up and down on his stool, the drummer sat on the left rear side of the band. The sweat on his large round face glistened on his dark skin. He had short, stubby black whiskers. His bass drum had the same design as the one on the fellow's shirt who had been at the door with the soon-to-be famous white cat. Up front just left of Yawdy, displaying a glistening smile from ear to ear, sat the banjo player. His wrist was a blur across the strings as he brought the banjo to life. His body alternated from side to side in the old wooden chair.

As the song wound down, the piano and drums kept a soft, light-hearted beat going in the background. Yawdy stood up to a round of applause, turned, and with his right hand acknowledged the band, as they all stood up and gave a bow. He smiled at the assembly in the room and said, "Thank all you folks for comin' and bein' here with us tonight. We are goin' to take a short break so old Cosmo can grease up that squawkin' trombone. If anythin' else falls off of it, we might just have to get him some balin' wire to keep him goin'. You're certainly welcome to stay with us. We'll strike back up in about twenty minutes."

It didn't take long for about half the place to clear out, and people to reposition themselves around the room. Two rows of tattered red and brown cushions spread across the floor in front of the band for informal floor seating. Of course, the whole affair was clearly on the informal side, and it didn't look as if there had been a paintbrush near the place for a hundred years.

Yawdy saw me standing against the wall, and hollered out, "Hey, Salty, you made it."

"Yes, I did, Mr. Rum. I couldn't pass on that free ticket."

"Step on up here, and I'll introduce you to my partners in crime."

I made my way through the thinning crowd and gave Yawdy's right hand a shake. "Yawdy, you never said you played in the band."

"Yeah, well, you never asked. Mister Mike, let me introduce you to the finest New Orleans jazz band in the world. Back here on the piano, we got Miz Ada Clark. She's the best darn ivory tickler in New Orleans."

"Hello, Ms. Clark."

"Why, Yawdy, what do you want from me? You ain't never said nothin' that nice before. Hi, Mike, nice to meet you."

"My pleasure, ma'am."

"I gave him my last free ticket, Ada. I figure if I started bein' nice, you might give me some more. Mister Mike, over here on the drums, we got Emmett Conroe."

"Hi, Mr. Conroe, nice to meet you."

"Likewise."

Yawdy continued, "This fella here on my left, on the banjo tonight, is Mash Fats."

"Hello, Mr. Fats."

"Yawdy said he'd done met someone from the salt mines over at Avery. Dat be you?"

"Yeah, I think so."

"Ol' Rum said you's a guitar picker."

"That's being kind."

"Well, where do it be, man? We always gots room for one more. Lord knows we need da help."

"I'm not sure I could even keep up, Mr. Fats."

"Mister Mike, our hard workin' cornet player is Zeb Cosner. Thinks he can play the clarinet and cornet both. We try to be nice to him so he don't take my place."

"Hello, Mr. Cosner."

"Ah, just Zeb, Mike. Nice to meet you. We ain't never met no friend of Yawdy's. Didn't know he had any."

"Gigi Louvier is our bass player. He really prefers the guitar, but we only let him play it on certain nights."

"Hi, Mr. Louvier." He didn't say anything, just flashed a quick thumbs up.

Yawdy set his clarinet down on the stand and turned to his right and introduced me to the final member of the band.

"Mike, this is Mr. Cosmo Thibodaux. Not many folks in the world can play the trombone like this ol' cat."

"Evening, Mr. Thibodaux."

He nodded his head, "Pleased to meet you."

You could tell Yawdy's band thoroughly enjoyed what they were doing. You could see it in their faces, the sparkle in their eyes, and the happiness they radiated. I guessed the average age of the band members had to be well over sixty-five. I hadn't seen anyone in a corporate position half their age with this much spunk. If I could only tap into that some way, wow, what would life feel like to be energized by your job?

"Ada, you remember Miz Goldie that used to play over at Pat's some?" Yawdy asked.

"Why, sure do, Yawdy. She was a ball. We used to call her 'hootie bird'."

"Well, she was a relative to Mister Mike here."

Ada looked at me and said, "No kiddin', how were you related to Miz Goldie?"

"She was my great-aunt. I didn't know her that well, mostly just talked to her on the phone a few times over the years. Always wanted to get down here and spend some time with her, but didn't get to."

"She was some great lady. Yawdy, didn't you run around with her old man?"

"Yeah, me and Amos had lots of good times together."

"How're your meetin's goin'?" Yawdy asked.

"Oh, just like always. When everything is said and done, more is usually said than done." He winked at me and gave a slight chuckle. "Yawdy, I'd like to buy you lunch and finish our conversation from the other night. I get done with my meeting on Friday, mid to late morning. Would you be available?"

"Wish I could, but we got a little gig over in Baton Rouge Friday. How about your next trip?"

"That might work. We have a brine project down at Port Fourchon we are working on. I'll be back in New Orleans in about a month, sometime in mid to late August."

Yawdy opened his wallet, pulled out a faded business card, and handed it to me. "Here, here's my card. My home number's on it. You find you're goin' to be back down here, you give me a call, and we'll set somethin' up. And don't forget to bring that guitar. We could pick out a few tunes together."

"You mean a lesson from a master?"

"Well, I ain't much of a guitar player, but I might have a tip or two you'd find useful. I might even have a thing or two I can share with you about your relatives. I got a story about ol' Amos you might like to know. Mister Mike, I'd love to sit here and jaw with you all night, but we gots to pay the light bill. You find you are goin' to be back down here, you be sure and call me now, hear."

"Yawdy, I'll be in touch."

I could tell he was serious about me getting with him. There was something about the way he looked at me, the way he listened when I talked with him, the way he shook my hand, and the way he paid attention to what I was saying. It was as if he could push back the outside world and make it feel like I was truly important to him.

SIX

An Office Window Gaze

"The greatest beauties of melody and harmony become faults when they are not in their proper place."

—Christopher Willibald Gluck

My black leather chair rolled a few inches away from my desk as I leaned back into it and let my eyes gaze out through the windows that ran from floor to ceiling the full length of my office. I had been in Minneapolis all week for meetings, and I'd found a few minutes to slip back to my office from the conference room. I stared past the white noise they pumped throughout the building, the vertical blue-gray miniblinds, and past the treetops outside my window to the cars whizzing by on the interstate. That's when I noticed it.

Hanging in front of me, between the miniblinds and the window glass, was a nine-inch-long wire and multi-colored glass creation my daughter made me years ago in one of her school art classes. The afternoon sunlight bounced off the sections of violet, crimson, orange, and green cut glass. It suddenly stuck me this simple creation hanging in my window was more than it appeared to be. It represented what often happens to creative talent within the confines of a large corporate organization, talent that must be subdued in order for a person to fit into the expectations of corporate culture. Here, in a few pieces of glass and copper-colored wire, suspended from a small clear suction cup, was a tiny representation of all of the creative opportunities, broken and bound by a corporate prison. The demands of a senior level management position, nearly constant travel, frustration with inept higher level corporate managers, and the intensity at home helping to raise an autistic child were all beginning to take their toll. More than ever, I began feeling the urge to make a significant change in my professional life. How long would it take to reinvent myself and set out in a new direction? I loved music, but not for a career. Startled by a knock at my office door, I spun my chair around to see who might be looking for me. "Oh, hi, Grantland, you haven't left for the airport yet?"

"No, I had a few things to follow up on after the meeting, and I wanted to ask if you were going to bring your running gear with you to Louisiana week after next."

"So you can run me by that ol' mangy German shepherd in the Quarter again."

"Hey, we can carry a stick next time."

"Come on in and sit down."

"I need to get your administrative assistant, Suzy, to call a cab for me."

"What time is your flight?" I asked.

"It's not till 5:30 p.m."

"Let me pack up a couple of things, and I'll be glad to drive you to the airport. I was looking for an excuse to leave a little early anyway."

"Mind if I talk while you're packing up your briefcase?"

"Nope, go right ahead. It'll just take me a minute."

"Mike, what's your opinion on the new business initiative that's underway?"

"You mean all the teams that are being formed to study and revamp all our business processes?"

"Exactly. Where are you on all of it?"

"We've worked together for a long time, maybe on and off for twenty-five years, huh? You want the party line or my real feelings?"

"You know me, the real version."

"We are overcomplicating our business. I understand the need to focus business processes around the customer, and the need to make sure all employees in the organization understand what's important to our customers. I'll even go along with documenting our business processes, but to take it to the level of minutiae we are…give me a break. We are mired in detail to a fault. That's where I get confused. I think everyone else does too."

"At end of the day, aren't we still in the salt business?" Grantland asked, with his eyes squinted as if he was trying to peer through a fog.

I closed down my computer and grabbed a number of files for work later that night. Grantland picked up his bag in the hallway closet, and we took the elevator to the parking garage. It was a little before 3:00 p.m. and looked like we'd beat the rush hour to the airport.

Grantland continued as we drove out of the parking lot, "The team I'm on met for the past two days discussing what was and wasn't a customer request! Talk about a waste of resources."

"Grantland, I've been around for a long time, and I've never seen such a complex business initiative in my life. I'm working harder than I ever have. And the worst part is I'm not convinced it's adding anything to the bottom line. I think it's all about our boss trying to look good to the higher ups at the very top of this organization."

"And, we are all paying the price!" he added.

"You got it."

"Mike, I didn't mean to dump on you. I know you are on the same page as those of us in the field."

"Hey, no problem. I wish I had some answers, but I don't. I often think it's time to look at what I'd really like to do in life, and move in that direction versus staying in the corporate environment."

"How about the writing?" he asked.

"I'm working on it."

"Are you still picking on that guitar?"

"Yeah, but I'm not ready for the tour yet."

"Didn't you meet a guy in New Orleans who played at Preservation Hall? Maybe he'd put you to work. You could pick at night and write in the daytime."

"Not in my wildest dreams. Besides, I'm not ready to move to New Orleans. I read a report last week on the barge industry and the Mississippi River system. It talked about what would happen if a major storm hit the city. The disruption in the shipments on the river would be nothing compared to what the article said the city would be up against."

"It hasn't happened yet. Some people say the voodoo keeps the hurricanes away," he added.

"Speaking of voodoo, do I need to prepare anything for the meeting at Port Fourschon?"

"No, not really, Mike. I'd just like to have you there to support what we are trying to get done."

"I can do that. What day do we start?"

"Monday afternoon for the tour of the port facility. You need to come in on Sunday to be there on time."

"Let me look at my schedule, and I'll let you know."

"What are we listening to on your radio?" he asked.

"It's a public station. They only play jazz and provide traffic updates. You like it?"

"Yeah, not bad. Sounds like we are in the French Quarter. When did you get so interested in the old New Orleans jazz?"

"I like all kinds of music, but after meeting that old jazzman in New Orleans, I've had an interest in learning a little more about the traditional music that originated there."

Light traffic on 494 allowed us to maintain sixty-five all the way to the airport. In just a little over twenty minutes we pulled up onto the upper level at Minneapolis-St. Paul International Airport main terminal building. As I pulled the car to the curb, I looked over at Grantland and said, "You know, I think we can all learn something from jazz."

"What's that?" he asked.

"First, things don't start off complicated; we make them that way over time. Second, life is supposed to be fun. And third, if you love what you're doing, you never get tired of it."

"Sounds to me like we could use a little jazz in the salt business."

"I think so. Have a safe flight. I'll see you in a couple of weeks."

He hopped out of the car and grabbed his bag. Before I pulled away from the curb, I reached into the back seat and pulled my planner out of my briefcase. I had slipped Yawdy's card into the pocket inside the back flap. I pulled out his card and dialed Yawdy's number on my cell phone.

"The salt guy, hi, Mister Mike, how are you?"

"Doing fine, and how about you?"

"Well, I been fightin' a little lumbago. You know anythin' about that?"

"Low back trouble, right?"

"Yeah. It's like carryin' an old catfish around and you never know when he's fixin' to horn you."

"Hope it's not too bad, Yawdy."

"Oh, just part of the gettin' old process," he added.

"Yawdy, I'm calling to let you know I'm going to be in New Orleans week after next for a meeting, and I thought I might come in a bit early and look you up. I'd even buy dinner. Are you available next Sunday night?"

He must have laid the phone down as I could hear the rustle of papers in the background. In a few moments he came back on the phone.

"Mister Mike, I can't find my calendar but the Hall is closed that night, so I wouldn't know why we couldn't get together. Where do you want to meet?"

"I'll come by your place and pick you up. And I'm sorry, I should have asked if your wife might want to go, too."

"Oh, no, Mister Mike, just me here. Are you goin' to have that guitar with you?

"Sure, I can bring it along."

"Come on by Sunday when you get to town and we'll see what we can do. I've got something in mind."

"Do we need dinner reservations anywhere?"

He didn't answer. *Well, I guess we'll just play it loose. They do call it the Big Easy.*

SEVEN

A Lesson from the Master

"Music is one of the greatest educators in the world."

—Anonymous

"Excuse me, I must have nodded off, did you catch what the captain said about the weather forecast for New Orleans?" I asked as I looked across the aisle to the forty-something sitcom-looking lady sitting in 4D.

She peered over the top of the frames of her hot pink reading glasses and answered, "I think the pilot said ninety-seven and scattered showers."

"Oh, boy, what am I thinking, going from Minneapolis to New Orleans in August? I must be nuts."

"I think all of us are," she added.

An every-button-in-place, muscular, dark-haired male flight attendant stopped the cart at my side. "Sir, will you be having lunch with us today?"

"Sure, what's on the menu?"

"Grilled chicken over rice or a vegetable medley with a marinara sauce. They both look pretty good."

"I'll do the vegetables. I'll get more than enough calories in New Orleans this week."

"Was that a violin I saw you bring on board?" he asked.

"No, it's actually an Alvarez guitar. It's a special travel size, so it's a little easier than carrying a full-sized one around the country."

"Are you playing in New Orleans?"

"Oh, no, it's just a hobby. I first picked one up when I was a kid and then gave up in frustration. About a year and a half ago I started taking lessons and found if I wanted to make any progress I had to have one I could carry on the road with me."

"Are you in the music business?"

"No. The salt business."

"Salt. You mean like table salt?"

"Yep."

"How do you make a living selling table salt?"

"That's only a small part of what we sell."

"You know, I think I've seen you before. Do you travel a lot?" he asked.

"Just about every week."

He placed the lunch meal tray containing the steaming yellow squash and green zucchini covered in a deep red marinara sauce on the tray table in front of me.

"Need anything else?"

"Just a little coffee, thanks."

We landed on time in New Orleans and taxied to the gate. It was a little after noon when the flight attendant opened the aircraft door to a steamy New Orleans' welcome. Shimmering puddles from an earlier shower covered the tarmac. Peeks of sunlight played with a sky full of billowing cotton-like clouds. Moisture condensed on the ceiling inside of the jetway and dripped steadily as I walked off the plane and into the terminal building.

After my customary fifteen minutes waiting at baggage claim and not a glimpse of my luggage, I made my way to the Northwest claim office.

"Good afternoon, how may we help you?"

"I just arrived on Flight #1435 from Minneapolis, and I am missing a bag," I remarked, as I handed the agent my claim ticket.

"You look familiar, or maybe it's the guitar."

"I was in here about a month ago with pretty much the same story. If you guys could keep better track of luggage, it would make my life simpler. I don't understand how you can lose luggage on a direct flight."

"Mr. Lane, it looks like your bag didn't make it on the plane. Right now, it's scheduled on the 3:45 p.m. flight. If you will let us know where you are staying, we'll have your bag delivered to you."

"I'm at the Saint Marie in the Quarter."

"Very good. If you will sign this receipt, we'll have your bag delivered to your hotel when it comes in. We're sorry about the delay."

I walked out of the lower level of the terminal building, hopped on the National shuttle van, and headed to the rental car lot. Except for two or three New Orleans area maps scattered among the seats, the rental shuttle van was empty. I'd been traveling for over thirty years in the course of my work, and yet I always felt the same, nagging, empty feeling when I had to leave on a Sunday. It was hard enough leaving Sharon at home to cope with raising an autistic child mostly by herself, but it was even harder leaving on a weekend. While I was feeling excited about getting to meet Yawdy again, I felt guilty for being gone from home.

"Ya'll have a great time, here in da city of Naw'lins," the rental car bus driver spouted over the intercom. "You's can pix up yo car anywhere in dis here aisle. Da exit is ova by da office. Do drive safely, Mister."

"Thanks," I said, as I stepped off the bus and up to the line of patiently waiting vehicles. I put the Alvarez and my briefcase in the back seat of a white Chevy Impala, and drove out of the lot headed for the hotel.

I enjoyed the drive downtown from the airport when I had time to take Airline Highway instead of hurrying along I-10. The New Orleans street signs conveyed a city unlike any in the country–Moisant, Guffrias, Labarre, Galvez, Dupre, Derbigny, Rampart, and on to Toulousse Street in the Quarter. Getting in early allowed me some productive time in my room at the Saint Marie to catch up on e-mail and finish the presentation I planned to give later that week in Detroit. It was too hot to get in an afternoon run and not having my luggage removed that distraction.

It was a quick five-minute drive from the hotel to Yawdy's. I turned onto Chartres Street a little after five. I spotted an empty parking space along the curb just past Yawdy's house. I locked the car, walked back along the broken sidewalk, and headed up the walkway to the wooden red steps on the left-hand side of the porch. The duplex was even more charming in the daylight than I remembered from the night I'd dropped Yawdy off in the rain. A greenish, orange moss grew along the edges of the old wooden shingles on the roof. The black hurricane shutters made it impossible to see in the windows. A beaming coat of new white paint covered the porch. It sparkled with the beaded raindrops left over from an earlier shower. A small bronze nameplate above the buzzer beside the door contained the letters *Y. Rum.* I pushed the button. In about a minute I heard the click from the bolt being turned in the lock. The door opened wide and through the rusty screen I could see Yawdy's bright eyes and his snowy bearded chin on the inside. His graying hair was slicked back, but wild, longer white hairs fanned out over his long, well-formed ears. I once read somewhere the Chinese believe full fleshy earlobes are a sign of a long, successful life. If that was true, Yawdy had many years to go.

"Right on time, Mister Mike, you must have had a good flight."

"Hi, Yawdy, good to see you again."

He pushed the screen door open and said, "Hey, man, where's that gig bag?"

"It's in the car."

"Well, hustle your fanny out there and get it. It's much too hot to leave it out there."

I walked back to the car, opened the door to the back seat, grabbed the Alvarez, and slung the strap over my shoulder. Yawdy waited on the front stoop.

"How was your luck with your baggage this trip?" he asked.

"Not too good. I'm starting to feel Northwest has it in for me. I'm hoping my bag gets here this afternoon."

The spring on the screen door creaked as Yawdy pulled it open. We stepped into the entry way and on into his living room.

I felt special to be invited into his home. His modest furnishings gave the place a homey feel. There was a matching brown overstuffed chair and sofa in the middle of the room. An orange, purple, and bright yellow granny square afghan lay folded over the back of the sofa. A four-shelf entertainment center stood against the far wall with a small television in the center section. The remaining shelves were loaded with pictures and figurines of all shapes and sizes, displaying a various array of musical instruments. An oval, multi-colored braided rug covered most of the floor in the living room. Scattered black quarter-notes decorated a yellowing shade on the lamp standing on the end table. The base of the lamp was made from a shiny black clarinet. An old ceiling fan made a clicking sound with each rotation above our heads.

"Here, set your instrument down right here on this chair," he said as he pointed to the overstuffed chair to my right. The arms on the chair showed years of wear as wiry white threads stuck out of the fabric. A tenor sax stood silently in a cradle at the end of the couch. An old black metal music stand stood nearby. The music stand had a small oblong music light clipped onto it with a frayed cord dangling off to one side.

"It's a warm one out there today. Can I get you somethin' to drink?" Yawdy asked.

"Oh, no, I'm fine, Yawdy, thanks. I moved the Alvarez alongside the front of the coffee table and sat down in the chair. Yawdy dropped onto the couch and put a pillow behind his back. There was a slight mustiness to the sultry air in the house and a faint background aroma of furniture polish.

"Looks like you are still having a bit of problem with that back," I commented.

"I'm a whole peck better than I was a few weeks back. I got me an 'ol chiropractor over on Basin Street, named Dr. Roy. He keeps my back blues under control. You're probably too young to know what I'm talkin' about."

"Don't I wish. Constant travel and sleeping in a different bed each night gives me fits. If it wasn't for routine back adjustments, I don't know what I'd do."

"That's good. Means you've learned to pay attention to what your body's a-tellin' you. Some folks don't know how to do that. I think our senses give us every clue we need to take care of ourselves. Our senses are a lot like the dynamics and tempo in a piece of music. They provide all the signs we need to keep the beat."

"Speaking of beat, Yawdy, how did you get involved in New Orleans jazz?"

"Oh, I guess I was just a kid. My dad died when I was five, and we moved in with my Aunt Gus and Uncle Benny. They lived next door to the old Saint Peter Baptist Church over on New Orleans Street. I used to sit out on the front porch and listen to the music coming from that place in the summertime when they'd have the windows open. Man, it'd be a rockin'. They had horns of all kinds, drums, guitars, and even a tuba.

"My Uncle Benny was a Methodist bishop. When we went to church, we sat with our hands in our pockets. It sure wasn't that way for the Saint Peter Baptists. I remember one evenin', I was sittin' on our front stoop listenin' to that music. My uncle came out, and sat down next to me. I said, 'Uncle Benny, what kind of music is that?' He said, 'Yawdy boy, that's a bit of heathen music, but it sure sounds good don't it?' I told him I wanted to join up with the Baptists, but he didn't think much of that."

"So that was your first brush with a bit of jazz?"

"Yeah, I guess you could say that. You know, Mister Mike, what most folks don't know is that jazz first came out of the churches in and around New Orleans. Storyville was the red light district, and I'm sure it had an impact on the early development of New Orleans jazz, but not near as much as the churches did."

"How's that, Yawdy?"

"Well, you see, you had the influence of the slaves and their music here in New Orleans. Then you had the Creole population too. They were a much better educated group of black folks. Many of the Creoles learned all about European music and its structure. I think the two came together in a worship settin', and the music grew from there."

"But don't many of the old jazz songs have a sexual reference in terms of the words?" I asked.

"Yeah, you could say that's the Storyville impact or just real life comin' through. Shoot, there's all kinds of sex in the Bible. Somebody was always begattin' somebody else," he chuckled as he leaned back against the pillow behind him on the couch.

"Yawdy, I've read that they credit some guy named Jelly Roll Morton as the father of jazz."

"Really it was Buddy Bolden, but no recordin's exist from his time. What's really funny is that jazz somehow got labeled as the devil's music."

"Why's that?" I asked.

"Well, somewhat because of the rumors about Storyville, but I think Bolden got his ideas from the Holy Roller church. It was a Baptist church here in New Orleans. But you know, music was such an important part of everythin' that happened in New Orleans, I imagine a little influence came from here, and a little bit from there."

"So when did you learn how to play?"

"My mom played the piano and gave lessons. She taught me and my brother how to play. When we was young'un's, our mom, Aunt Gus, and Uncle Benny hauled us around to play at different churches. They were always goin' to meetin's of some kind or another."

"That had to be a great experience."

"Yeah, it was. I never got my height until I was in eleventh grade. I was always real short for my age. Shoot, folks thought I was five or six years old when I was nine. They used to say, 'man, look at that kid go.' Ha."

"So did your mom teach you how to play the clarinet?"

"No. I had an old music teacher named Furst Manassas. My lessons were on Saturday, and old Mister Manassas liked to drink more 'en just a bit. Shoot, one week he'd tell me the F key was on the right, and then the next week, he'd tell me it was on the left. I had a heck of a time, but I finally learned it. I taught myself how to play the saxophone. It's really my favorite instrument, but I always play the clarinet in a jazz band. I play the cornet some too. Say now, we are not helpin' you on that guitar. Get it out and let's see what you are doin'."

I reached over, got the Alvarez out of the zippered gig bag, pulled the electronic tuner out of the pocket, and tuned up. Yawdy had taken his sax off of the stand, attached it to a leather strap around his neck, and sat back down on the sofa.

"Ah, heck, I can't play on this soft pile of mush. Let me get a chair."

Yawdy got up, walked across the room, and grabbed a wooden high back chair, pulled it over next to the coffee table, and made himself comfortable.

"My goodness, Yawdy, sounds like you can play about any kind of instrument. I'm just a neophyte on all this."

"You know any jazz, Mister Mike?"

"I've got the sheet music with me for 'Polka Dots and Moonbeams.' Will that work?"

"Well, it ain't New Orleans jazz, but if you've been practicin' it, we can sure play it."

"I can do something else, if you'd rather," I offered.

"No, that's fine. Grab that stand and set your music up there where you can see it. What key are you going to play it in?"

"I think it's an F."

"In bar sixteen, you goin' to change to an A? There is normally a key change there."

I looked at the music and counted out the bars.

"Yes, it does. Pretty good, Yawdy. Sounds like you already know this tune."

"They used to call me the walkin' fake book, Mister Mike."

"A fake book. What's that?"

"It's a music book that only contains the chords and melody line. Works in a pinch. You got to know the bag."

"The bag?" I asked.

"What do I have to do, man, teach you the lingo, too? The bag, the bag—melodies, improvisation, how to interact with other instruments, and even what to wear."

"You might have to start at square one with me, Yawdy."

"Okay, let's swing it. Pick it up on one, the second time through." He began counting. "One and two and three and four and one…"

He took off on the melody line, so I could follow. He was being nice, because he slowed way down for me to keep up on the chord changes. After a bit, he pulled away from the sax, and started singing.

"The music started and I was the perplexed one. I held my breath and said, may I have the next one? In my frightened arms, polka dots, and

moonbeams sparkled on a pug-nosed dream," he sang, then went back to the sax, and as effortlessly as ever, picked up the melody. It was as if he could project himself and his emotion through that shiny old horn. It was all I could do to keep going. I felt I sat in the presence of a master who was leading me, step by step. I lost track of the number of times we played through the song. He must have stopped a dozen times to help me understand the chord progression.

"Mister Mike, sit right there and don't move."

Yawdy got up and put his horn in the stand. He came over to me, put his right hand on my left shoulder, and added just a bit of weight. He was wearing a black cotton T-shirt and black slacks. The manner in which he was dressed made his white Fu Manchu, and the color in his face stand out from the rest of his appearance.

"You feel that?" he asked.

"What's that?"

"The tightness in that shoulder."

I tried to focus on my shoulder to get a feel for what he'd said.

"Yes, I think so. Am I holding it too high?"

"No, just too tight. Let it go. Put your conscious awareness right there in that shoulder and tell it to relax."

I followed his instructions, as my shoulder dropped about an inch and a half, and my elbow came back closer to my side.

"Now, does that feel better?"

"Yeah, it does."

He kept his hand on my shoulder, grabbed my right wrist with his left thumb and index finger, and raised and lowered my hand a couple of times, all the while holding it just off the strings.

"Let that wrist go, just like your shoulder. Put your awareness in that wrist and tell it to relax."

I could feel the muscles in my wrist release.

"That's it. Now, you can play like that all night and not get tired. You'll sound better, too. You'll feel the music. Just like we was talkin' when you came in about payin' attention to your senses to take care of them ol' back muscles. I said it was a lot like the dynamics and tempo in music. Your body is feedin' information to your brain all the time, but you just gotta be listenin' for it. Mister Mike, you have to use your attention, sense what's goin' on in your body, and make the changes to get rid of the stress and the tension."

He stood back and looked at me. I didn't know what to say. I felt different. The guitar felt good in my hands; it felt natural.

"So, it's not just about paying attention to the music."

"Oh, no, it's more than that," he said, as he looked down at the sheet music lying on the coffee table I had pulled out of my bag. "Hey, 'The Crawdad Song.' Can you play that?"

"Sure, but it isn't jazz."

"Maybe not, but we can jazz it up a bit. Plus, we call it the crawfish song in Louisiana. Ain't no one down here eats a crawdad! You ever eat any of them crawfish, Mister Mike?"

"Oh, yeah, I've had them a few times over the years."

"Well, there ain't nothin' no better than a fresh crawfish boil."

He took off singing, sounding like Louis Armstrong, and I worked on my strumming to keep up.

"You get a line, and I'll get a pole, honey. You get a line, and I'll get a pole, babe. You get a line, and I'll get a pole, and we'll go down to that crawfish hole, honey, baby mine..."

It was a little after 8:00 p.m. when I looked at my watch. We'd been at it nonstop for a bit over three hours. I could tell he loved music. He moved with every song. He created a beat you could follow. He came on and off of the sax like it was a well-worn saddle on a mount he had ridden all his life. He switched back and forth between playing the saxophone and clarinet with total ease. He explained things, but mostly he talked about my attention, using it to rid the tension in my body, so I could express the energy of the music.

"Yawdy, what do you say we go grab a bite to eat? Is there some place you really like to go? It's on me."

"Have you ever been to Elizabeth's?"

EIGHT

Elizabeth's in Marigny

"Music is the essence of order and leads to all that is good."

—Plato

We parked on Gallier across the street from a turn of the century, two-and-a-half story white clapboard building. Fading black paint trimmed the windows and shutters on the old structure. There appeared to be an apartment or some type of living quarters on the second floor. We walked to the corner entrance at street level and stepped inside. The scent of Cajun spices and rich dark chicory coffee permeated the intimate café.

It was a little bigger than a small coffee shop, and the place was packed, but not with diners from the Quarter. These were local folks—couples, families, older people, and neighbors of all sorts. The square tables throughout the café stood draped with brightly colored orange, blue, and green plaid tablecloths. Hand-painted Cajun pictures adorned the walls all around the dining room.

As we stepped into the café, we were greeted by the hostess. She was an attractive woman, maybe thirty, with coal black hair, and the creamy white skin of French ancestry. She wore a pinkish, red apron with her name, Rachel, written in a fancy script across the top. The apron covered a white cotton dress that went to the top of her ankles.

"Evenin', Mr. Yawdy, we haven't seen you for a few days. Where you been?"

"Oh, my ol' lumbago been actin' up, Rachel. I just been lyin' low."

"Who've you got there with you?" she asked as she looked my way.

"This is Mike; he's a friend of mine from Minnesota," Yawdy answered.

"Hi, nice to meet you."

"Mister Mike, this here is Rachel. She can't find no other job, so I come down here to make sure she's got someone to practice on."

"Why, Yawdy Rum, didn't your momma tell you, you was supposed to be nice to ladies?"

"Excuse me there, Rachel. I must've forgot."

"How about that. Beautiful thang like me comes along an ol' Mister Yawdy be forgettin' all his manners."

Yawdy just stood there looking at her, flashing his wide grin.

Rachel reached out and grabbed him by the chin whiskers. "What's the matter there, Mr. Yawdy, you been blowin' on that ol' clarinet too long?"

"Rachel, you gonna pick on us all night or find a table so a couple of hungry fellas can get a bite to eat?"

She pulled two menus from the rack by the door, turned, and led the way to the far side of the room.

She continued the affectionate bantering. "Sorry, Yawdy, if I'd known you be comin' here with a guest this evenin', I would've had a fancy name card waitin' for you."

Yawdy looked at her and winked. "Rachel, I'll ring you up next time," he said.

"Enjoy dinner, gents."

Yawdy sat down on a squared-backed, blue wooden chair with his back to the wall. I pulled out a matching yellow one and sat down facing him. Tall, skinny bottles of red spicy Louisiana hot sauces adorned the center of the table. The small glass salt and pepper shakers seemed meek in comparison.

"So, Yawdy, on the way over here you started to tell me about Amos and Goldie. You said my Aunt Goldie played the piano some at Pat O'Brien's. Is that how you got to know her?"

"No, I got to know Amos first. He was an oilman. He worked for one of the big service companies. He was always entertainin' clients and settin' up big get-togethers. When he did, I took care of the music for him."

"At Preservation Hall?"

"We did a few events at the Hall, but mainly I'd get a group together for a gig on a riverboat, in a meetin', or some special dinner he was puttin' on. He loved New Orleans jazz."

"And Goldie?"

"Well, one night our piano player took sick, and we needed someone to fill in at the last minute. We couldn't find a soul. So, Amos said, 'Let's ask Goldie.'"

"She agreed?"

"Yep, she jumped at the chance. Said she wanted to keep an eye on the ol' goat when he was out gaddin' around, and bein' in the band would work perfect. Don't know where she learned about music, but, man, she had some kind of ear for it. I sure did get a kick out of Amos. We went fishin' a few times over on the rivuh, but mostly it was business. After he died, Miz Goldie stayed pretty active. She was a good seamstress and did all kinds of sewin' in her home. She mended several things for me over the years. They lived up the street from me on the corner of Rue Marigny. Mister Mike, I wish I could tell you more about your family, but I'm not sure there's much more to tell."

"I appreciate learning what you've told me, Yawdy. I should have taken the time to look her up when I was first down here years ago. But, as I told you, I guess I was always in too much of a hurry to plan some extra time into my schedule."

"Well, I'd say you learned somethin'."

"What's that?"

"I don't think you was in a hurry this afternoon. The main thing about life is to learn as you go along and make adjustments in who you are and who you want to be."

He reached over to the edge of the table and pulled a small wicker basket covered with a bright red napkin closer to the center.

"Here, get some of this here corn bread, it's better than anythin' you'll get up North."

Our waitress stepped up to the table and said, "Evenin', Mr. Yawdy, how are you?"

Curly jet black hair encircled her face. She didn't look much over twenty-one. Her skin color reflected an even closer lineage to the French.

"Just fine, Miss Diane. How are you doin'?"

"Perfect."

Yawdy gave her a quick wink.

"If I was as young as you, I'd be perfect, too. What's your special tonight?"

"We have an Asian pu pu platter. It comes with spring rolls, stuffed chicken wings with piquant sauce, plus a half a stuffed catfish, and homemade coleslaw. Servin' shrimp gumbo for the appetizer. How's that sound?"

"Works for me. Mister Mike?"

"Sounds good."

"Yawdy, have you tasted Rachel's new Abita Amber Chardonnay? It's really good," the waitress commented.

"Mike, you up for a sip?" Yawdy asked.

"I wouldn't pass it up."

She glanced at the wicker breadbasket on our table. "Looks like you are good on the corn bread. Let me turn your order in and get that wine."

Yawdy spread butter across the end of a piece of corn bread and took a bite. "Mister Mike, tell me about your family."

"Well, my wife, Sharon, and I have three kids. Our oldest is a girl. Her name's, Tauna. She's twenty-six. Then, a son, Taylor, twenty-five. Our youngest is nineteen. His name is Patrick. He's autistic. He still lives at home with us. Probably will for quite a while."

"How long you been married?"

"Almost thirty years, and she hadn't run me off yet."

"What's autism like?" Yawdy asked with a puzzled look.

"It's a mystery in many ways. Some say it's like your brain is wired differently. Life is very concrete for an autistic person. You go making any changes in the routine of someone who's autistic and you're asking for a hard time. It's really a disorder ranging across a wide spectrum. I've often told my wife I think we are all autistic, just at different points on the continuum. Patrick is one big puzzle."

"I don't really know much about autism, but I imagine your wife has her hands full with you being gone all the time," Yawdy said, as his face tightened a bit.

"I tell people she's a saint. My goodness, what she goes through in order to keep things on even keel at home. If I didn't have her, Yawdy, I'm sure I couldn't do what I do, what with all the traveling and such."

He let his face broaden into a wide smile. His caring brown eyes were intently fixed on me, "Mister Mike, we all got a different place to play in the band, and we sure do need the others, don't we?"

"No doubt about that."

He picked up his knife, took a swipe at the butter, and spread it across the end of the piece of corn bread he was holding in his left hand.

"Yawdy, if you were going to explain jazz, how would you do it?"

He sat there for a couple of moments without saying a word. He closed his eyes and puffed out his cheeks like he was gathering air for the first note of a riff on his horn.

"Dependin' on what you are talkin' about, there is a lot to explain. You know, there's all kinds of jazz. You got Dixieland, Harlem, Kansas City, Chicago, the cool stuff that grew up in California, and what we play, traditional jazz. That's what many folks call New Orleans jazz. Which one are you askin' about?"

"I suppose jazz at its most basic level. Would that be New Orleans jazz?"

"I'd say so. To me, jazz is spiritual. It's about the rhythm of life. It's about the creative energy that flows through all of us."

"But it's still more than that, isn't it?"

"Well, sure. There's the whole musical technique side of it. If you are goin' to understand jazz, you need to know a little about music theory, the way harmony works, rhythm, improvisation, instrument technique, and things like that."

"But some musicians play totally by ear, right?"

"Sure, and they're darn good, too. But to really know what's goin' on, you need the technical side as well."

Our waitress brought the chardonnay and placed the glasses on the table.

"Here, Mister Mike, how about a toast? Here's to the mysteries of life, to tryin' to learn a little each day, to findin' somethin' for each of us in each our own way, and to you and me sittin' here tonight, may we not drink so much that we both go home tight!"

Yawdy tipped up his glass and took a sip, and I joined him. The chardonnay was like butter with a blend of the best sweet oak and a hint of citrus.

"I read somewhere that jazz is about the musical instrument emulating the human voice. What's the story behind that?" I asked.

"We express emotion in our voices, don't we? My guess is the human voice existed long before anyone created an instrument. When you're playin' jazz one of the most important aspects is to put the emotion of the song into the instrument to convey feelin'. It's not just about hittin' a note, it's about creatin' emotion by bendin' it, gravelin' it, screamin' it, whisperin' it, and cryin' it. We do that with our voices all the time, don't we?"

"Sure, but we don't really think about it; it just comes natural."

"There you go. So tell me a little about the salt business. Where did the salt come from that's here in south Louisiana?"

The world of traditional jazz, as Yawdy framed it, seemed fresh and interesting. I wanted to learn more about jazz, more about New Orleans, and Yawdy. I felt frustrated having to talk about the salt business. I liked just two friends getting to know each other. Oh well.

"Have you ever heard about plate tectonics?"

"Nope. Sounds like it's got somethin' to do with your dentures."

I chuckled. "No, I don't think so, Yawdy. Over millions of years, a salt formation got deep enough and under enough pressure, it bubbled up through a fault line that runs along the Gulf coast. Kind of like when you squeeze modeling clay in your fist and it oozes out between your fingers. When you drive towards Avery Island on 329, and you look south, you can see the rise in the surface of the earth, nearly two hundred feet on top of the salt."

"How'd the salt get down there in the first place?"

"It was originally deposited when an inland sea evaporated millions and millions of years ago. Then over time, geologists believe, it was covered up with sediments and volcanic material."

"How did they find out there was salt over at Avery?" he asked.

"Native American people probably discovered the first salt springs in the area. The Avery mine is one of the oldest in the country."

"Well, shut my mouth. What's all that salt used for?"

"Most of it goes for highway de-icing up North."

"You ever been down in the mine at Avery?" Yawdy asked, as his eyes opened wide.

"Oh, yeah, several times."

"Didn't you tell me, you go over a thousand feet down, to get the salt?"

"Yes, I did. Today, we are mining at about sixteen hundred feet. I could probably get you down there sometime if you wanted to go."

"No way, man. I didn't drop nothin' down no hole I need to go after. I think this ol' cat would just be better off stayin' on this side of the grass."

We went back to the feast set before us. The shrimp gumbo tasted superb, but it paled in comparison to the pu pu platter. Yawdy didn't waste a minute getting his share.

"Yawdy, you're a pretty lean fellow, how do you eat like this and keep the weight off?"

"Ooo eeee, livin' in Louisiana, with all this good food is mighty tough. If a fella don't watch it, those pounds can really add up. I had a problem with it at one point in my life."

"You look like you are in great shape today."

"Yeah, I'm pretty good for being eighty-one."

I could have fallen out of my chair. Here was a man as full of life as anyone I've ever seen. I'd guessed he was in his early to mid seventies. But eighty-one years old? No way!

Yawdy continued. "I had a problem with my weight when I was younger, but I learned to get it under control. Shoot, I was even over two hundred and fifty pounds at one time."

The waitress brought a fresh basket of the corn bread and replaced the one on our table.

"Yawdy, did I hear you tell him you were eighty-one? Why, I think you're every bit of a hundred."

Yawdy snapped back. "Actually, two hundred, Miss Diane. Had you fooled, ha."

"Yes sir, Yawdy Rum, plum fooled me. You guys need anything else? Maybe some coffee?"

Yawdy looked up at her, and said, "Now, Miss Diane, you ought to know a guy over a hundred has got to have his beauty rest. Coffee this time of night wouldn't do me any good."

She looked my way. "How about you; I suppose you need your beauty rest, too?"

"Do I look a hundred?"

"Well, now anyone runnin' around with this ol' coot ain't no baby."

"I'll do a cup. I've got enough e-mail I need to work on tonight, some good chicory coffee should help get me through it."

"Dessert tonight? We've got homemade bread pudding."

"Not me. Between the gumbo and catfish, I'm stuffed," I deferred to Yawdy.

"No, Miss Diane, just a check when you get time. Thanks."

"So, what was the answer, Yawdy? How did you take the weight off?"

"Just started payin' attention to what I was eatin', same manner as I told you to put your awareness into that shoulder and hand when you were strummin' that guitar this afternoon. It's amazin' what will happen when you finally start payin' attention to what goes in your mouth. Take a meal like this one tonight. It's not a problem to take in a little extra, you just can't eat every meal like it was your last, or before long it will be."

"I think there are a lot of folks today who could use that advice, Yawdy."

"Sounds too easy, don't it?"

"Sure does," I said.

"You know what, though? It works."

I sensed he knew something about life, something that allowed him to overcome obstacles that trip up most of us. He knew something that gave him insight into improving himself. He seemed happy with himself and at ease with his surroundings. He looked relaxed. Many of us are not that way. We are all tied up in knots trying to cope with life, trying to deal with the demands of a job or career, family, financial issues, health, and all kinds of other stress.

"Yawdy, have you ever been married?"

"I was once, but she died a long time ago."

"I'm sorry."

"Oh, no reason to be sorry. That's just how things work sometimes. She was carryin' twins and somethin' went wrong with the pregnancy, and I lost her."

"And the babies?"

"Lost them, too."

"Any other children?" I asked.

"Nope."

"Married only once?"

"Yep. Got close a couple of times, but guess I never did meet the right gal."

"What was your wife's name?"

"Della. She was a pretty lady. I really loved her; guess I still do. They say a person never falls out of a love that's cut short."

I finished my cup of the rich, black coffee and took care of the bill. A steady, light rain shower fell as we walked kitty corner across the street to where we parked the car. It seemed to have cooled off a bit as well.

"I could walk home from here. It would do me good," he offered.

"That's okay, Yawdy. I have to pick up my guitar at your place anyway. Hop in."

We pulled up in front of Yawdy's place, and I went in with him and gathered my things.

"Mister Mike, are you goin' to be around here all week?"

"I have to go down to Port Fourchon tomorrow, but I'll be back here for meetings Tuesday and some sales calls on Wednesday morning. I have to be in Detroit later this week; why's that?"

"Well, you asked me about jazz. Have you heard of Louis Armstrong Park?"

"Sure. It's up on the back side of the Quarter."

"There's a curved bench just inside the front entrance off Rampart. It's just a bit off to the left side of the main gate. Can you meet me up there Wednesday afternoon about three?"

NINE

Congo Square

"Jazz came to America three hundred years ago in chains."

—Paul Whitman

It was about a quarter to three, when I made a U-turn on Rampart Street at Saint Phillip. Louis Armstrong Park ran several blocks along the back o' town side of the French Quarter. I slipped the Impala in behind a sun faded red pickup parked along the curb a few car lengths past the main entrance gate. I dug into my briefcase until I could come up with enough quarters to feed the meter glaring at me from the curb. The afternoon sun glistened off the deep green, waxy leaves on the magnolia trees and made the whole area feel like a greenhouse.

There, just inside the gate, as Yawdy had described, stood a curved, black wrought iron bench cooling itself in the afternoon shade. I scanned the area both inside and outside the fence along Rampart Street, but didn't see Yawdy anywhere. I reached into my back pocket, and pulled out my airline ticket. My flight was at 7:25 p.m. I glanced at my watch and figured I needed to be on my way to the airport no later than 5:30 p.m. to make my flight. I sat down on the wrought iron bench and felt the strength of the metal bands support me. Just as I leaned back against the warm iron work, my cell phone rang. Caller ID displayed Sharon's number.

"And what are you up to?" I asked.

"Oh, I had a few minutes and I thought I'd see if I could catch you. Are you on your way to the airport?"

"No, not yet. I'm waiting to meet Yawdy. My flight isn't until seven-thirty. I should be home a little after ten."

"Don't you turn around and leave again?"

"Yes, to Detroit. I leave at 6:30 in the morning."

"You might as well just sleep at the airport," she said with a sigh. "With you leaving early last weekend, it seems like you've already been gone a week."

"What's going on there?" I asked.

"We miss you."

"I miss you too."

"Patrick woke up grumpy. Nothing suited him this morning."

"Any idea why?"

"I think something is going on at school, but he won't say what it is. I met his new case manager yesterday. She's going to do some checking for me. She has a background in autism and developmental delays."

"Did she offer any insight as to what might be going on?"

"No. And as you know, it's often impossible to make sense out of what's going on inside that boy. I think I need a trip somewhere, and you can stay home with the grind around here. You feel like you're trapped in your job; you should try mine."

"There are times I wish we could change places."

"Oh, yeah, you'd last a couple of weeks, and then you'd be wanting back out on the road."

"I might surprise you."

"I gotta go pick Patrick up at school. Fly safely, and call me when you are headed home from the airport."

I must have drifted off as I sat there on the bench because I never heard or felt him sit down next to me.

"Catchin' you a little catnap, 'eh?"

My eyes popped open, and I squinted into the light at the figure sitting next to me. "Afternoon, Yawdy, I must have snoozed off."

"Late night last night?"

"Yeah, I was up late working on a presentation for a meeting in Detroit tomorrow."

"Man, you travel more than the band at the Hall does. Do you ever spend any time at home?"

"Not enough. My wife, Sharon, doesn't think so either. I just hope my dog remembers me when I walk in the door."

"How long did you say you been in the salt business?"

"Thirty-three years, Yawdy. Long time, huh?"

"No, not really. I've been playin' jazz for over seventy years."

"Ah, but you love it, right?"

"Oh, yeah, Mister Mike, that I do, but I gather you like the salt business, too."

"A person has to make a living, do something to put a roof over their head. The salt business has been good to me and my family, but I wouldn't say I love it anymore."

"Why's that? Because of what the business is extractin' from you?"

"Yawdy, when I was in college I needed a job. That's when I started working in a salt mine in Kansas. Over my career, I've been in almost every phase of the business. But today, more than ever, it has come to the point where it consumes all my time."

"But you are one of the bigwigs, right?"

"I'm the vice president of sales and marketing."

"How many rungs on the ladder between you and the guy at the top?"

"Within our division, one. I report to the president."

"You want his job?"

"At one time I thought I might, but as I've gotten closer to the top I don't see anyone having any fun. And it seems the harder you work, the less they appreciate you."

"How's that?"

"Well, you get to a point where you have to carry the party line, whether you agree or not. Oh, you hear those above you say they want your comments and input, but I'm not sure they really do. You are expected to act in a certain manner that fits with their expectations. If you rock the boat, you're in trouble."

"Mister Mike, are you rockin' the boat?"

"I get a little ornery. I tell them what I think. I get things out in the open. I cut to the chase. I let my passion for things show."

"And that gets you in hot water. You don't fit the mold."

"Yeah, you could say that, if I ever did. I think I finally got to a level where I either fit the mold or get out."

"What's at the root of it?" he asked.

"I'd say two things, Yawdy. First, I have no respect for the fellow I report too. He's just not someone I'm ready to charge up the hill with. But more than that, I'm not getting younger, and I'm realizing that if I'm going to achieve my personal goals in life, I need to make a change."

"Then you feel the business isn't tappin' into your full potential."

"I hadn't really thought about it in those terms, but I guess you could put it that way. I've told you I've always wanted to write a book."

"Why don't you do it?"

"Up to this point, I've never felt I had the mental energy after dealing with all the issues in my job and my family."

"So do you have any options?"

"You mean like leave or go do something different?" I asked.

"You would have to tell me." Yawdy got up from the bench and said, "Come on, Mister Mike, follow me."

We walked side by side, silently for about five minutes, along winding sidewalks, over an arched white concrete bridge, and into the center of the park. Yawdy led me off the walkway out onto a deep green grassy lawn. We stopped under the shade of a towering palm. The fragrance of fresh cut grass filled the air. I could hear the hum of mowers in the distance.

"The other night at Elizabeth's, you asked me how I would explain jazz. I think it's best to bring you here, and let you experience the very birthplace of it all. Mister Mike, here's the spot. There was an edict called the Code Noir that prohibited slave owners from workin' slaves on Sundays. The slaves who lived in New Orleans could gather here. New Orleans afforded them a bit greater level of tolerance and freedom than any other location in the South."

"A maid at the hotel referred to this place as Congo Square. I suppose that's why?" I asked.

"Yes. You gotta understand black folks lost everythin' they had when they were uprooted from Africa and transported to the new country. Everythin'. Everythin' except for one–their music. Yes, sir, yeah, music. They brought their music from their homeland here. That's all they had. Imagine black men, women, and children gathered in a circle, with rudimentary instruments–drums, sticks, stringed instruments, bones, glass bottles all joinin' together, creatin' a syncopated, pulsatin', rhythmic movement, accompanied by the voices and chants that lived in their collective souls."

Yawdy slowly made a turn as he stood next to me. His eyes were closed. He must have been describing the scene he was seeing in his mind. Maybe, in some way he was connecting with his heritage.

He continued, "And they danced. Some say an African line dance called the Calinda and the Bamboula."

"Yawdy, are you saying that was the first jazz?"

"Not exactly, I believe it was more the creative energy that brought jazz to life. I heard this fella one time givin' a talk on the subject. He used the term 'syncretism'. I think it means the blendin' together of two cultures."

"But New Orleans offers a blend of many cultures," I added.

"Oh, yeah. There were French, Spanish, English, Acadians, and Native Americans all here together. Just look around, the ethnic diversity is still here."

"And you're saying, with it a greater level of tolerance, to explore, and create."

Yawdy looked at me straight on. "Some call it the Africanization of American music and the Americanization of African music. I believe, it was a blendin' of the discipline of European musical structure with the free form of native African music. Jazz is the embodiment of the creative energy that began with the slave dances that happened here where we are standin'. And it happened here because of the tolerance that existed. Multi-cultural tolerance and respect to a point. You have to remember they were still slaves."

"I'm hearing you describe this emotion-driven, boiling cauldron of humanity mixing with the steamy atmosphere of New Orleans, coming together in a way unlike any other place on the planet."

"Bingo."

"That's why you said, 'spiritual', when I asked you the question the other night at dinner."

"It don't get no more spiritual than that, Mister Mike. Many folks called early jazz the devil's music because they thought it came from the bordellos in the district. I've spent all my life immersed in New Orleans jazz. From what I know, ol' Buddy Bolden got his inspiration from the house of God, namely, the Holy Rollers."

"That's the church you said was next to your aunt and uncle's house."

"Nope. That was the Saint Peter Baptist Church. Shoot, they couldn't hold a candlestick to the Holy Rollers."

"Did you know Bolden?"

"No, I didn't. He died when I was about six, but he hadn't been around here for years. They say the bottle got the best of him, and he ended up bein' put in a mental institution in Jackson. Some say he was the best cornet player ever. Course ol' Bolden never played with Satchmo."

"Satchmo, wasn't that Louis Armstrong's nickname?"

"Yep."

"Any of Bolden's recordings exist?"

"There are rumors about some he made that got lost, but nobody knows if that's true."

"How about sheet music he might have written?"

"Mostly head music."

"Head music."

"Here I am again, havin' to teach you everythin'. Ain't you never heard of head music?"

"I don't think so, Yawdy. Remember I'm not from New Orleans, and I'm just learning about jazz."

"Well, for all anyone knows, most of ol' Bolden's music was stashed in his noggin. It got passed on from one musician to another. Some of the ol' timers said the Holy Rollers had more jazz in their music than a New Orleans dance band, only it was probably more vocal."

"How did the association with the bordellos in the district come about?"

"You can pick up any piece written on New Orleans jazz and find that most all of the early musicians played in the red light district. Jelly Roll Morton is one you might want to read about some time, when you ain't got nothin' to do. He was probably the first real composer of jazz."

"Yawdy, did you know him?"

"No. I didn't know Mister Jelly Roll. But I've known lots of other jazz musicians and all of them willing to help you out anytime you'd ask. I think they wanted to make sure the music passed on to the next generation. Mister Mike, one musician learns from another. One person will take another's technique and perfect it a bit further. Take a riff, or improvisation, and noodle around with it in a new different direction—harmony and rhythm mixed in new and expanded ways. You had all these musicians workin' together, some in the bordellos, others playin' at funerals and family get-togethers, and often at church mixed with black spirituals."

"So the energy from this place, the influence of the church, and the creative genius of people like Bolden and Jelly Roll launched jazz."

"Yes, and lots of other folks, too. I could recite names for you all day long."

"And you said the connection with the bordellos in Storyville added an additional influence on the music."

"Oh, don't you know it. Just take a look at some of the titles of the early tunes—'The Black Bottom Stomp,' 'Creole Love Call,' 'The Empty Bed Blues,' 'Funky Butt,' 'Need a Little Sugar in My Bowl,' 'Four or Five Times,' and 'You Got to Give Me Some'."

"Pretty mild compared to some of the music today," I offered.

The afternoon sun dropped behind a line of billowing, puffy cumulous clouds. I could feel the stickiness in the late day air.

"Yeah. Mister Mike, I'd say some of today's music is a bit on the raunchy side. You're lookin' at your watch. You gotta head to the airport? Come on, I'll walk with you back to the gate."

We headed across the lawn to the sidewalk we had followed into the park.

"Yawdy, do you think the creative energy that brought jazz to life here in this place is still active today?"

"As much as ever. And I think it's equally available to each and every one of us. No one person or group owns a lock on the power that brought jazz to life. When you think about it, somethin' amazingly powerful grew out of somethin' horrible."

"But I think you'd agree some of us have an easier time connecting with the musical side of that creative power than others."

"Maybe, some folks are just a little more in tune to it."

"Yawdy, your playing seems so natural, so much a part of you. You make it look effortless. I have to work my tail off for months, just to be able to play one song, and then sometimes, my wife still can't tell what it is I'm playing."

"Mister Mike, how long have you been really workin' at music?"

"Seriously for about two years, but on and off for a lot longer."

"You said you had been in the salt business for over thirty years, right?"

"Yes."

"Well, if I was to watch you in your job today, I might say you make it look easy. But, if I was to observe you after you had only been in business a couple of years, I'll bet I'd be watchin' a person with a much lower skill level. Agree?"

"Okay."

"You have to put your musical interests, skills, and knowledge into perspective."

"But, Yawdy, back to the creative energy we've been talking about this afternoon with jazz. How do you think a person finds out what will unleash the energy in themselves?"

"What's your passion?"

"I think I know, but wouldn't say I'm 100 percent certain."

"Well, you gotta get certain. You find your passion, and I can share the secret of how to get where you want to go. Just like the folks I told you about this afternoon who used to come here and sing and dance. When they lost everythin', they found they had somethin' more powerful still within themselves–their music. Maybe music isn't your natural gift. You say you want to be a writer. If you put your effort into writin' a book, I think you'll tap into some creative energy you may not even know you possess. I told you that night we was sittin' together on the airplane that a composer has to write down the score to bring a tune into bein'. The same is true for you or me if we really want to achieve a goal we have for ourselves. We have to take that goal out of our noggin and get it down on paper."

Yawdy turned, placed his black beret at a slight angle on his head as we stopped just outside the front gate along Rampart. A crowded city bus, filled with afternoon commuters, roared by us in the street.

"Yawdy, you got a degree in psychology?"

"Nope, just a degree in life."

TEN

Back to the Quarter

*"Jazz is the only music in which the same note can be played
night after night but differently each time."*

—Ornette Coleman

The agent confirmed my suspicions: the flight was canceled and my
only workable option for Detroit was early the next morning. I grabbed
my briefcase, the Alvarez and my roller bag, and headed for the taxi
stand. The fingerprint-smudged glass doors closed behind me with a
whish as I stepped out of the terminal and into the line of weary looking travelers waiting in the cab line. The clip snapped as I released my
cell phone from its holder on my belt, popped it open with my thumb,
and called Sharon.

"Did you get back early?" she asked. It's just a little past 9:00
p.m."

"No. I'm still in New Orleans. They experienced a mechanical
problem with the plane."

"So what time do you get in?"

"I don't. I'm booked on a flight in the morning to Detroit."

"Well, that's just great. I think I might have my bags packed when
you get here."

"What's up, dear, issues with Patrick?"

"Yes, he had a blow-up today at the school. I guess some kid was teasing him after lunch, and this wasn't the first time so they got into a fight."

"Did anybody get hurt?"

"Patrick got knocked down. He's got a black-and-blue eye and a few scratches on his face. I don't know about the other kid. The regular teacher was gone, and the substitute didn't know the procedure with Patrick."

"So what did she do?"

"She called the principal, and the police liaison got involved."

"Oh, crap. Didn't they know they were dealing with someone with autism?"

"Oh, crap, is right, and the answer is no."

"So what did you do?"

"I had to go to the school and get him. There's a meeting tomorrow to sort things out."

"What can I do?"

"Nothing from where you are. When do you get home?"

"Mid-afternoon on Friday."

"After tomorrow's meeting about Patrick, I'll know more details and can fill you in when we talk tomorrow night."

"I'm sorry, dear. I really wish I was there."

"Thanks, I wish you were here too, but you're not. This job of being a mom gets pretty tiring with all the issues here. I've gotta go. I love you, dear."

A helpless feeling came over me every time a situation like this developed and I was on the road. The distance made it impossible for me to do anything other than listen and attempt to relate to whatever she was trying to handle. Feeling sorry for myself not being there never helped. I'd found over the years, I couldn't dwell on what was going on at home and still be effective at my job on the road.

I didn't have the heart to tell Sharon I was thinking about scooting back into the Quarter. Yawdy told me that Gigi was going to do something special tonight on his guitar at the Hall. He'd asked me if I could stay. Maybe I'd run back into the Quarter, take in some music, and grab a bite to eat. I caught a taxi with a stale, smoky, cigar smelling aroma to the hotel, checked in, dropped my bags, and in less than twenty minutes was back in another cab headed for town.

"Where do you want go in the Quarter?" the cabbie asked.

"Preservation Hall, but you can drop me off at Bourbon and Canal, and I'll walk in."

"You here on business?"

"I have been. I was supposed to be headed back to Minneapolis, but there was a problem with the plane, so I ended up here an extra night. I hope to take in a bit of jazz and grab a bite to eat."

He snapped back, "I don't care for New Orleans jazz; it's too tinny sounding for my ears."

"I think it has to grow on you."

"I'm from Russia. I've been here for about two years, and it ain't grown on me yet."

"You're a long ways from home."

He raised his eyes and glanced at me in his rearview mirror. He had a long, red scar along the right side of his face. There was a hurtful, discomforting look to it.

"New Orleans is now my home, but I don't like it here."

"I suppose you could drive a cab about anywhere," I offered.

"I don't have any money. You have to have money to have options. That's why I'm working. I'm trying to save up a nest egg to move my family to Chicago, but it is hard because it takes everything I make just to pay the bills. I'm trapped in this steamy place."

"At least it sounds like you have a plan," I said.

"I hear of many immigrants who come to the United States and make big money, but I don't think they drive cabs."

The traffic was heavy, all the way back into the city. I glanced at my watch. It was 10:08 p.m. I hadn't thought about calling Yawdy and letting him know I was going to be around for an extra night. I just hoped I could get into the Hall. With an early morning flight staring at me, I wasn't going to stay out late. The cabbie swung around the median on Canal and pulled up to the corner of Canal and Bourbon streets.

"They put the barricades up at night, so you gotta walk from here. You know where you need to go?"

"Sure, just down river a few blocks. Good luck on your plan to get to Chicago, and thanks for the ride." I handed him the fare and a new crisp five-dollar bill for a tip, slid out of back seat of the cab, closed the door, and stepped around the barricade blocking traffic from Bourbon Street.

The street had become a walkway for the throng streaming into the Quarter for the evening. Street musicians lined the sidewalks all along the block. Each had staked out a claim to a section of the walkway in the hopes of generating a steady cash flow into all kinds of cans and old beat-up instrument cases lying about them on the ground. From the humped over figure of an old black gentleman in a wheel chair wailing away on a severely dented trombone to a group of kids beating out a rap progression on plastic buckets and metal cans, the sidewalks offered it all. The sounds resonated in the alley way and against the buildings in the hot night air. The vibration made my eardrums pulse with the pounding beat.

I could only imagine what it would be like to be here during Mardi Gras. I'd heard lots of stories over the years. It would have to be a madhouse.

Even though it was early, there were groups of people standing in the streets looking up at revelers on the balconies and ironwork railings all along both sides of Bourbon. Young men on balconies waved strings of Mardi Gras beads as they taunted the females in the street below. I stopped just past the corner of Bourbon and Saint Louis streets, where ten or twelve ladies in the street were bantering with some young men perched on a balcony.

"Show us somethin'," a young fellow kept hollering from up above. "Ah, come on, show us somethin'."

"You show us somethin' first, honey," one of the women yelled up to the balcony. Sure enough, as I looked up, one young man pulled down his pants and offered the ladies an eyeful. The group in the street exploded with laughter and then about half of the young women grabbed their tops and pulled them up to chin level. A bombardment of beads rained down on the street.

I made my way around the throng and on to Saint Peter Street where I turned by the entrance to the Krazy Corner bar. Next door, Ali Babas looked packed with visitors clamoring for fresh gyros. The sweet aroma of the fresh baked lamb filtered out onto the sidewalk.

I was taken back when I noticed the line stretching down the sidewalk from the entry to Preservation Hall. There was a small mob pressing the doorway. I walked out into the street and on to the end of the block where the line of jazz hopefuls snaked back up river along Royal Street.

I crossed the street and stopped near the doorway of Reverend Zombie's Voodoo shop so I could get a full view of the front of the Hall. A voice behind me spoke out.

"I think they are bringing them out of the woodwork tonight."

I turned around. It was the shopkeeper I encountered the first time I visited the Hall. She had the same black scarf tied around her neck, and her glistening black hair was tied into a ponytail with a bright green bandana. She was maybe thirty, about five feet, three inches, with pretty dark olive colored skin.

"I think it is a little too popular for me tonight," I said.

She was staring past me towards the Hall, "I like the old building, don't you?"

"The place certainly has character. Looks like it could use a little paint though."

"The building is as old as jazz itself. It was built as a home in the mid 1700s. It was a tavern during the war with the British, and it survived the 1816 New Orleans fire."

"You sound like you really know about the place. I thought you were in the voodoo business."

"I am," she said as she looked back across the street. "The Hall has been a butcher shop, a clothing store, and even a doctor's clinic. I think it has been mostly artists' quarters for the past hundred years or so. It wasn't known as Preservation Hall until about 1960."

"How do you know so much about the place?"

"The wife of the man who started the Hall is a friend of mine. She and I spent a lot of time together. We've talked about the place for hours. I've got a relative who plays over there as well. There was even a two-story slave quarters that bordered the patio in the courtyard. We used to talk about the spirits that lived within its walls."

"You mean ghosts?"

"No, just all the spirits who have been preserved by the warmth of the place."

"Preservation Hall, I guess that's an appropriate name."

She looked at me with deep, penetrating brown eyes. "Very appropriate. I think you should take the gris-gris home with you. You never came back the last time I saw you here."

She handed me a small shiny, silver charm. It was a miniature guitar.

"How much?" I asked.

"Six dollars."

I pulled the ones out of my billfold.

"What does the charm stand for?"

"Well, you must like music."

"I do."

"It will bring you good luck."

"Thanks, and thanks for the history lesson as well. I'm sorry I didn't catch your name."

"I never offered it." She extended her right hand. "I'm Adrian."

We shook hands. "Nice to meet you, Adrian. My name's Mike. Have a nice evening."

I looked back across the street to the Hall. The old building was jumping in place with the heartbeat of jazz. There was a faint yellow hue on the hurricane shutters from the light radiating through the glazed windows. They were rocking inside, and I didn't have the time to stand in line to get in. The Hall wasn't going to work for me tonight. I stood there a few minutes, then decided to walk back downtown via Bourbon Street.

Just around the corner from Saint Peter Street a young, thin, muscular African-American boy, I estimated to be about fourteen, sat on the curb next to a boom box. A cardboard beer flat lay in the gutter in front of him. Wrinkled ones, fives, tens, along with an assortment of coins covered the bottom of the box. I noticed him dancing in place on the sidewalk a few minutes earlier as I headed to the Hall. A steady stream of sweat ran off his forehead and down his jaw line from the heat he had generated with his sidewalk tap dance. He gave me a strange look as I sat down next to him on the curb and watched him counting the money he had earned from those who stopped to watch him dance.

"Looks like you are having a good night."

"Yeah, why, you a cop?"

"No, just a businessman. Looks like you are doing better than I am, though."

"Little better than most."

"Pretty good crowd here tonight?"

"They are turning loose of their dollars; that's good," he said.

"You dance here like this on the sidewalk very often?"

"Three or four times a week."

"Make much?"

"Three, four hundred on a good night."

"No kidding."

"You ain't a cop, are you?"

"No, I told you I wasn't a cop. Where did you learn to dance?" I asked.

"On the street, but it's something that's just inside of me. I found people would pay me for what I could do with my feet."

"Ever take any lessons?"

"Some."

"Help?"

"A bit."

He continued counting the money as he emptied his beer flat. He placed all the tens, fives, and ones in order and began gathering the coins from the box.

"How did you learn you could dance?"

"I guess I just felt it. You ever hear music that made you want to tap your foot? Of course, you're a white guy, so maybe not."

"I've heard a beat that made me want to tap my foot."

"Did you tap it?" he asked, in an almost confrontational manner.

"I tapped it. Sometimes, I move my whole body as well, depending on the song."

"Well, I move my whole body, too, and I'm going to keep moving until I make enough money to go to college and study dance. I'm going to be somebody someday."

"I think you already are. My name's Mike. What's yours?"

"Honi. My mom named me after the famous dancer Charles 'Honi' Coles. He was the greatest. He learned to dance on the street, too."

He folded the bills around the coins and dropped them into a pocket in a backpack nestled tightly in his lap. Then he placed the backpack in the beer flat, grabbed the boom box, and stood up.

"You sure you ain't no cop?"

ELEVEN

Getting Home

*"No art is more connected
to the inner life of mankind than music."*

—Ritter

I reached into the side pocket of my briefcase and pulled out the CD I'd purchased from the news shop at the airport before I left New Orleans. *Preservation Hall Jazz Band Live!* I chuckled as I removed the tight, clear wrapper off the case. There was a picture of the band on the front cover—six older musicians all in white dress shirts and business looking neckties radiating New Orleans charm. And none other than my old friend, Yawdy, sitting in the center of the photo with an ear-to-ear grin.

The flight attendant stopped next to my aisle seat but not before almost taking my arm off at the elbow with her beverage cart.

"Care for something to drink?"

"Do you have any wine left?" I asked.

"I've got a Gallo Cabernet, but it's hot. The ground crew stowed it next to the meal warmers for first class. It will be five dollars if you want one."

"I think I'll do a Coke instead."

"I've got Pepsi," she responded.

She dropped two ice cubes into a small plastic glass, poured what was left over from an open can, and handed me the glass. There was no way I could get the tray table down, so I just held on to the cup. I was being crushed against the aisle side armrest from the middle seat passenger who looked more like a sumo wrestler. When he got on the plane I was already seated. I obliged when he asked me to raise the armrest on the right side of my seat. I thought he'd lower it once he sat down, but with his size I should have known better. I thought about charging him for half of my seat.

I thought of the young man I'd met Wednesday night on Bourbon Street. He said he was pulling in three hundred a night, and he danced three or four times a week. Heck, that boy could be knocking down nearly five thousand a month, not bad for a fourteen- or fifteen-year-old kid. I doubted if he really understood the significance of knowing what he wanted to do with his life. Maybe he was one of the lucky ones with a clear sense of where his life should go at such a young age. I never did. I don't think most people do. Shoot, here I am nearly forty years older than the kid on the street and still wrestling with the issue.

I thought about Yawdy. I wondered if his musical goals and interests were firmly set in his mind at a young age. I hadn't asked him that question. Had he ever wanted more for his life than playing at Preservation Hall? Not that there was anything wrong with that. Were Yawdy and Honi somehow equal in the clarity of purpose they felt for themselves at a young age? Did I have a clear picture of what I wanted to do with the rest of my life? More importantly, did I have the courage to follow my passion? How much longer could I continue playing the corporate game?

I popped the CD into my Discman and slipped on the headphones. The music came to life. I closed my eyes. I listened to that spicy beat of traditional New Orleans jazz and its steady rhythmic pulse—a heartbeat, the heartbeat of New Orleans and Congo Square. It contained simplicity and innocence.

Yawdy said with New Orleans jazz every instrument plays the melody and supports the rhythm as well. Seems like that is a good comparison to our own lives, we each carry the melody of life and support the rhythm of every living thing on this spinning planet.

I breathed a sigh of relief when I could finally get out of my seat and stand up after we taxied to the gate. The sumo wrestler looked like he was going to need a crane to get out of his seat. I wasn't certain if the lady against the window was still breathing. My back felt like it was in a vice from the way I'd been sitting all bent out of shape. I'd been gone from home six days. Someone once said to me, "Man, all the traveling you get to do by jet, I'll bet it's great"–*yeah, right. What a way to travel.*

The belt on the baggage carousel was spinning when I rounded the corner from the escalator and walked past the security guard. I'd hoped with being one of the last few people off the plane my luggage would be waiting when I got to baggage claim, but no such luck. I checked voicemail while I waited. There was a message from my assistant, Suzy.

"Mike, we've received the confirmation on the dates for the next distributor meeting. I'd like to talk to you early next week on the location. It looks like New Orleans will work better than Baton Rouge and is slightly lower cost. I'm working on the arrangements for transportation and entertainment for the group. I need to talk to you about the jazz contact you've got down there."

Bags began coming down the slide onto the carousel arriving with a thud as they hit the base. I wondered if we could talk Yawdy into firing up the band for a group of crusty ol' salt distributors. My roller bag, black like every other bag on the carousel, popped though the opening and shot down the baggage slide. I flipped the phone closed, grabbed my bag, and headed for the parking garage.

It was a quick drive home. I turned off the blacktop and onto the freshly graded dirt roadway of the cul-de-sac. We were lucky to get one good grading job a year out of the township crew. It looked like they had just finished. I pulled into the driveway and got out of my car. The late afternoon summer sun shone down through the cottonwood trees in the front yard and danced off of both stories of the house. The light tan siding seemed to move with the flickering light.

Sharon was standing at the sink when I stepped into the kitchen. She turned and wiped back her bangs from her forehead. She was as pretty as ever in her red cotton tank top and khaki shorts, her frosty gray hair, her slim, shapely frame, and her bright smile. We embraced.

"I got your message. Thanks for letting me know you were going to be late. How did your presentation go in Detroit?"

"I got through it, but not without ruffling a few feathers."

"Tell me what happened," she replied.

"The operations guys don't want to admit we've got a quality problem with our shipping procedures. I'm not going to sugar coat how we stack up against our competition. I tried to give them the facts. That's not what they wanted to hear. Talk about a bunch of thin-skinned prima donnas. So, how is it going here?"

No more had the words left my mouth, when a door slammed upstairs, and I saw frustration come over Sharon's face.

"Patrick?" I asked.

"Oh, yeah. He's not having a good day. He's loaded for bear. The fight at school resulted in a week's suspension. I'm not sure he understands the situation he's gotten himself into. Maybe you can talk to him."

"I'll go up and see what I can do."

When I opened his bedroom door, his favorite teddy bear, Contrary, hit me in the face.

"Whoa, what's going on, Patrick?"

"LEAVE!" he shouted.

"Hey, buddy. It's good to see you."

"LEAVE!"

"I hear it's been a tough week. Do you want to talk about it?"

He swung his feet off the edge of the bed, stood up, and wrapped his arms around me. His five-foot, ten-inch frame nearly matched mine. He was almost a man, yet he was still a very young boy. One of the biggest challenges understanding Patrick's autism was the rapid mood changes. It was as if a switch flipped something on and off inside of him.

"I missed you, Dad."

"I've missed you too, Patrick. Want to talk?"

We spent the next thirty minutes or so trying to reconstruct the story of what happened at school. In one breath the other boy started it all, then comments about the school, then Mom, then his bear, then his bicycle, and then he let me know that was enough talking and he wanted me to leave. That's often how autistic conversations go, hither and yon with indecipherable connections. I never got the full story of what had taken place.

I walked back downstairs to the kitchen and stood next to Sharon at the sink. "Did you sort things out at the school as to what happened?"

"Not really. It's turned into a mess. As I told you on the phone, the regular teacher and his paraprofessional were gone when everything happened. The substitute teacher was inexperienced with special needs kids and wasn't sure how to handle the situation."

"Do you suppose Patrick told the substitute the other kid was picking on him?"

"I doubt it. Patrick doesn't advocate for himself," she responded.

"So he probably never said anything to the substitute."

"Right. If you are autistic, the substitute isn't the teacher, she's the substitute."

"So did the she get the principal involved instead of his case manager?"

"Yes. And the police officer who's assigned to the school. His name is Tom. He is concerned about Patrick's best interests and in getting the facts, but I could tell he didn't know a thing about autism."

"So where do we go from here?"

"We are going to have to go to court."

"Court, what for?"

"Patrick is going to be charged with disorderly conduct."

"But you said you didn't think he started it."

"We really aren't 100 percent sure who started what. The other boy is going to be charged with battery. I've had to follow up with Patrick's dean, his case manager, the regular teacher, the principal, the therapist, the police, and the county prosecutor this week."

"Wow! I'm really sorry you've had to deal with all of this on your own."

"Well, it goes with the territory. I can give you the dates you'll need you to put in your planner so you can be here for the court hearing and help sort everything out."

"Does the prosecutor know he is dealing with a special-needs person?"

"I have a call in for him to discuss Patrick's disability. Boy, it's nice to have you home to share the load." Sharon continued rinsing the radishes she was sorting out in the sink. "Now, tell me about your trip." she asked. "Did you get to meet Yawdy on Wednesday?"

"Yes, we met in Louis Armstrong Park. He gave me an education on jazz. The history is quite fascinating. I think there is something I'm supposed to learn from all of it."

"You mean about music?"

"No, not just music, more than that, I think something about life, about discovering my passion, pursuing it, and not being afraid to follow my heart."

"Well, if you figure it out, you know I'll support you. I think you would be happier than you are now. You've said you are not having fun anymore in the salt business."

"Thanks, dear. That means a lot to me."

"But I'm not going to have to *listen to that music,* am I?"

TWELVE

The Creole Queen

"Come sing me a bawdy song, make me merry."

—William Shakespeare

I'd been in Louisiana for most of the week playing host for our annual distributor meeting. It was a pleasant November evening under a cloudless sky with the temperature in the sixties when I parked the rental car on the bumpy gravel lot. My shoes were dusty by the time I walked across the lot to the boarding platform to the old riverboat. As I stepped on board, I could feel a gentle rocking from the waves blowing across the Mississippi. Yawdy stood just inside the doors on the main level.

"Well, Mr. Rum, what do you think? Are you ready for a night on the river?" I asked.

"Oh, don't you know it. We're set to start stompin' when your group gets here. The band boarded a little earlier and had time for a little woodshed work."

"I thought you guys didn't need to rehearse."

"Hey, now, don't go and tell anyone. You'd ruin our reputation."

"I'll keep the secret. Yawdy, is the brunch event at the Hall still on for Sunday?"

"Sure is. You gonna be able to make it, aren't you?"

"From what you told me, I wouldn't miss it. I'll come over to your place and pick you up."

"And you're still coming over to my place tomorrow for a bit of pickin' as well, right?"

"I sure planned on it," I responded.

Yawdy leaned a bit to the left, and peered around behind me. "Looks like someone is lookin' for you."

I swung around, and glanced back toward the entry way. Coming up behind us was my administrative assistant, Suzy, who had just boarded the boat. Suzy was a fire cat and the tint of red in her hair proved it. We'd worked together for many years. Although she was barely over five feet tall, she never missed a thing when it came to meeting planning and group entertainment.

"Hi, Suzy, is everything in order?" I asked.

"Yes, it is."

"Yawdy, have you met my sidekick? She's my right arm for these types of events. Suzy, this is Mr. Yawdy Rum."

I could tell Yawdy was taken back by Suzy's stature. She barely came up to his mid chest. I could also tell from the grip she had on his right hand, she was asserting her authority.

"Hello, Mr. Rum. It's a pleasure to meet you. Mike has told me all about you."

"Oh, no. I'm in trouble now."

"What I'd like to know is if you are able to teach him anything about playing the guitar?"

"Well, I'm tryin' but, you know, Mister Mike's a bit of a slow learner."

"Oh, yeah, don't we all know that. Gents, our first load of guests are just pulling up in the bus now. Mr. Rum, if you'll get your group going, we can welcome these folks on board this magnificent old riverboat."

Suzy spun around and headed back towards the door on the boarding level. Yawdy looked at me as he massaged his right hand.

"Damn, she's got one heck of a grip. Does she always shake hands like that?" Yawdy asked.

"You ought to see what she can do if she doesn't like you."

"Mister Mike, we just want to say thanks for askin' us to do this with you. It means a lot to all of us in the band. We love keepin' this music alive."

"You're welcome, Yawdy."

Yawdy turned, and walked through the double red and white swinging doors into the dining room of the *Creole Queen*. Moments later the sound of New Orleans jazz exploded from inside. I walked back to the entry door of the old paddle wheeler and helped Suzy welcome the group we'd spent the last three days entertaining. That's really what these events had turned out to be. Oh, we'd held a meeting to discuss business strategy, but the time together was more about building relationships than anything.

A dinner cruise on the Mississippi River with Yawdy and the Preservation Hall Jazz Band made a perfect ending for what had shaped up to be a successful meeting with the group of distributors. The hospitality of the people of south Louisiana, Cajun cuisine, and the energy from New Orleans jazz made it easy to put folks at ease.

After dinner, I stood near the rear doorway watching the lights go by from our viewpoint on the river. An earthy mustiness filled the air from the chocolate waters churning in the Creole Queen's paddle wheel below the deck. A light spray floated off of the wheel as it made its steady revolutions. I felt a tug on my left sleeve and turned to see Suzy standing next to me.

"How did you meet him?"

"Who, you mean, Yawdy?"

"Yes."

"I think it was five or six months back. We were on a flight together from Minneapolis. We both lost luggage, and I ended up giving him a ride home."

"How old is he?" she asked.

"Eighty-one."

"No way!"

"Amazing, huh?"

"I guess," she added still looking quite surprised.

"He's full of energy. He's full of ideas. His mind is sharp. It's like every cell in his body is alive and young." I added.

"How's he do it?"

"Probably good genes, but also I think it comes from living out his passion. And, it's not just Yawdy; look at the whole band. It's like they're busting at the seams with life."

"They are energizing."

"That's an understatement," I added.

"Mike, are you going to do anything over the weekend besides work?"

"As a matter of fact, I am. On Sunday, there is an event at Preservation Hall Yawdy invited me to attend with him. I guess the musicians who play at the Hall and their families get together from time to time for a private brunch and a jam session. It should be interesting."

The group inside continued dancing to the invigorating beat of New Orleans jazz as we neared the pier. They had connected with the music. Or perhaps they were just trying to work off dinner. Both were probably the case. I walked outside the main entry door and watched one of the deckhands getting the mooring line ready for a tie-up at the dock. His tennis shoes squeaked with every step he took on the wet decking of the old riverboat. The sparkle of the lights of the city of New Orleans stretched out below us.

"How much higher are we than the city?" I asked.

"'Bout ten feet. Bein' here on da rivuh gives a fella a diffent viewpoint, don' it?"

"Sure does. Have you ever been here in a bad storm?"

"Yeah, lots of 'em ova da years. Dey say dat da whole city wud be unda water if'n da big pumps quit."

"Let's hope they never do."

"I cares, but I don' cares. My house is up high, built on stilts. If'n it don' blow away in da hurricane, I be just fine. Watch out dere, mister, I's gots to trow da line."

The old riverboat kissed the mooring and snuggled in close. We had to get the band to shut down in order to get the group headed for the buses. Once they were loaded and on their way, Suzy and I walked back on the boat to make sure everything had been taken care of.

"Ms. Suzy," Yawdy hollered. "We had a special song for you, but we never did get to play it."

"Well, I'm all ears," she replied.

Yawdy turned to the band. "Pick it up, Emmett."

On the drums, in his wrinkled white dress shirt and flashy maroon and blue speckled bow tie, Emmett Conroe began counting. "Okay, kids, from the top, one, two, three, four…."

The tune was "Five Foot Two, Eyes of Blue," but they had changed the words a bit.

"Four foot two, eyes of blue, but oh! what those four foot two could do, Has anybody seen my girl? Turned up nose, turned down hose, Never had no other beaus, Covered with fur, Diamond rings and all those things, Betcha' ol' Suzy ain't any taller than her."

"Why, Yawdy Rum, you are a dog, and so is your band."

"Suzy, I think they like you," I commented.

"Oh, yeah. Well, I'm every bit of four foot three, so there."

It took less than twenty minutes for the band to dismantle and pack up their instruments. Not long after, we were standing at the bottom of the gangplank to the boat as they loaded their gear into an old green and red twelve-passenger Ford van. Yawdy and I stood next to each other, waiting for everything to be loaded up.

"Say there, Mr. Rum, that day you and I were in the park, you said something to me about a secret."

"I did?"

"Yes, you did. You said if there was something I wanted to change in my life, you would share a secret with me as to how to achieve it."

"Well, if you are still comin' over tomorrow, I suppose we could have a little talk then."

THIRTEEN

Sweet Tea

"Music is the inarticulate speech of heart, which cannot be compressed into words because it is infinite."

—Richard Wagner

Saturday morning's always have held a sense of freshness for me. Maybe it's because the pressure of the workweek has subsided. The clear mid morning sky provided a crisp blue backdrop for the golden glow of the leaves in the hackberry trees along Chartres Street. I parked the car across the street from Yawdy's, reached into the back seat, grabbed the guitar case, and a black portfolio containing several songs I'd been working on. As I crossed the street, I noticed a small-framed fellow in white khaki bib overalls on his hands and knees trimming a stubby little green holly hedge along the front of the porch. He looked to be much older than Yawdy.

"Howdy."

"Howdy. You lookin' fo dat Mister Yawdy?"

"As a matter of fact I am."

"He ain't bein' no where 'round here."

I glanced at my watch. "It looks like I'm a little early. I suppose I can just grab a seat here on the front stoop and wait for him."

"Well, dat might take a spell. He wudn't feelin' too good when dey took him to da doktor dis mornin'."

"Doctor?"

"Yep. His niece come by here, and she be takin' him wit her."

"I hope it wasn't serious."

"I wudn't know 'bout dat one way or da udder. Just know dat Mister Yawdy wus bent ova a bit when dey left."

"Do you know where they went?"

"No, but dey sed someone by da name of Mike wus goin' to stop by, an he'd be carryin' him a geetar. I bet dat be you?"

"Yeah, that's me."

"Well, here be da phone number dat his niece left. I tank it be her cell phone. Lord knows Yawdy don't got one."

He reached into the front pocket of his overalls and handed me a folded piece of paper. I held it open and read the phone number scrawled on it.

"Thanks. Are you Yawdy's gardener?"

"Ah, I just be doin' a bit of fix-up stuff fo him. He always be tellin' me to watch da safe when he's gone."

"Safe?"

"Yeah, ol' Yawdy's a hoot. Always tellin' me he been havin' dis safe in da cellar all full of loot. Old coot don't I know, he ain't even got no cellar!"

"Thanks for the information. I'll give the number a call."

"You're welcome, mister. Y'all be havin' a nice day."

I walked to the rental car, opened the back door, and put my things inside. Doubled over? Had Yawdy gotten some bad food on the *Creole Queen* the night before? I think we all ate the same thing. I hoped that was all it might be. And, niece, he never mentioned he had any relatives. I recall him talking about a brother at one point. Maybe he had some kids who lived in the area.

I pulled out my cell phone and dialed the number.

"Hello."

"Hello, this is Mike Lane. I'm calling for Yawdy Rum."

"Oh, hi, Mr. Lane. This is Yawdy's niece. He mentioned that you would probably call. He said that y'all were meeting at his place."

"Is everything okay?"

"Yawdy's feeling better now. I'll let Yawdy give you the details. He's right here. Hold on just a minute."

A soft rustling came through the speaker as she put Yawdy on the phone.

"Hi, Mister Mike, sorry I messed up our lunch. I had them fried oysters all ready to go."

"Yawdy, are you okay?"

"Oh, just a little problem with my plumbin'. I think I'm fine now. In fact, I'll be home later this afternoon. You can stop back over then, can't you?"

"Be glad to Yawdy if you are feeling up to it. Anything I can do or get for you?"

"Oh, no, I don't need nothin', just come on by. And, Mister Mike, don't forget to bring that guitar."

"Are you sure?"

"Yep. I'll talk at you later."

I closed the cell phone, started the car, and decided to run a couple of errands. It was nearly 4:30 p.m. when I pulled back up in front of Yawdy's. It looked like his yard work had been finished. I stepped up on the porch and rang the buzzer. It took several minutes for him to answer the door.

"Hey, how you doing, man?"

"At my age, as long as I'm on the right side of the grass, I'm doin' fine. Come on in."

I stepped in the doorway and sat the guitar case just inside the door. He still looked a bit pale.

"Are you feeling okay?"

"I'm sure better than I was earlier today. Damn."

"What's up?"

"Well, they tell me I have a cancer. I guess it's in my prostate gland. A while back the doctor gave me some pills for it. They were sure pricey little devils. So I decided I make 'em stretch a bit."

"You cut back on the prescription?"

"Just a titch."

"And your problem came back."

"Yeah, how do you know? You got the same thing?"

"No, I've just read a bit about it, and I've had several uncles who've had to deal with prostate cancer. Did you have the PSA test?"

"Did I have what test?"

"PSA."

"If that stands for I couldn't piss any, I had that test. I couldn't go a drop."

"Have you had surgery?"

"Not the major surgery, I had the implant where they put the radioactive seeds in the prostate gland. Shoot, I was in and out of the hospital the same day, kind of sore afterwards, though."

"You looked fine last night."

"I guess I shouldn't have cut back on the pills. They keep every-thin' flowin' okay, if you know what I mean."

"Yes."

"So I had to have my niece take me down to the doctor so they could tap the keg."

"And what did he tell you?"

"He told me to take the pills as he prescribed, come hell or high water."

"I guess you'll be following his advice."

Yawdy looked at my guitar sitting against the wall. "Hey, you got a bigger case. What have you got in there?"

"Something new. Wanna see it?"

"Open it up man. Let's take a peek." I laid the case over on the floor, opened up the clasps, and removed the guitar.

"Ooooo weeeee. That boy went and bought him a Gibson, and an AJ at that! Let me hear somethin'."

I sat on the arm of the sofa and strummed a few bars of the "On the Sunny Side of the Street." Yawdy was shaking his head back and forth as he listened.

"Man, listen to the tone that little darlin's got."

"You know, Yawdy, when I hold it, I feel like it's capable of so much more than anything I can do on it."

"What'd I tell you?"

"Practice, right?"

"Mister Mike, you know what a repeat symbol looks like don't you—the heavy black bar on the musical staff with a fine line and two dots either before or after it, depending on where it appears in the musical score."

"Well, sure."

"I learned long ago that symbol was one powerful tool. From a practical standpoint, if you are the composer it saves writin' the same section over. You can just have the musician repeat a section. If you are the musician you don't have to keep turnin' pages to play a piece you don't know by memory. But, the repeat symbol and what it stands for is more than just a musical tool. If you are tryin' to change or improve somethin' in your life, you gotta repeat the desired behaviors, you gotta practice, stay in tune, and work at it till you get it right. It applies as much too important things in your life as it does to makin' music. Now, that Gibson, well, it's just a tool. If you repeat your practice and keep on repeatin' till you get it right, you'll accomplish what you've set out to do with your music. The same is true for your life. You want somethin' to drink? My niece made up some sun tea before she left."

I followed Yawdy through the house to the kitchen where he got a couple of tall aluminum iced tea glasses out of the cabinet. One was Christmas tree green and the other plain aluminum. I remember my grandmother having the same metal glasses. They sweat like crazy anytime you put something cold in them.

"There's ice in the fridge. I hope you like sweet tea."

Yawdy stepped out through a laundry room at the back of the kitchen, pushed open the screen door, and leaned out onto the back porch. The door swung back shut with a bang. He came back in with a glass gallon jug filled with fresh tea. One inch yellow and green bands circled the middle of the clear glass jug.

"She puts the sugar in when she sets it out in the sun, does a body good."

"So I take it that your brother had children."

"Yeah. Butch had a boy and a girl. One of 'em lives here, and the other in California."

"Does your brother live in New Orleans?"

"No. He passed away about three years ago."

"Was he a musician, too?"

"He played up till he was a teenager, but not as an adult. Thought it was too hard a way to make a livin'. Here, sit down, Mister Mike. Tell me what's been goin' on. We didn't get any time to talk last night, and it's been a few months since you were here."

Yawdy pulled out a chair from the kitchen dinette. The shiny chrome frame encircled the red Naugahyde on the backrest and seat cushions. The table had a slate gray top with a turquoise and pink boomerang pattern in it.

I ran my fingers across the top of the table. "My parents had a table just like this when I was a kid, only the chairs that went with it were yellow."

"Yeah, it's an old one. What were we talkin' about?"

"Your brother. You said he didn't stay in the music business."

"You see, Mister Mike, it hasn't been that long ago that as black musicians we had a much tougher time gettin' work and when we did, we were on a lower pay scale. If'n you couple that with end of prohibition and the radio, things just got pretty bleak in this country for black musicians."

"Prohibition and the radio?"

"Durin' prohibition, folks went out to speakeasies to get a drink and listen to live music. There were lots of jobs for musicians in those days."

"And they went away after prohibition?"

"A person didn't need to go out to a club to get a drink. You could buy it legally, stay home, and listen to music over the airwaves. Radio stations came on the scene in the twenties. Folks didn't want to listen to darkies as we were called."

"What about Louis Armstrong? He was popular wasn't he?"

"A few made it, but most didn't unless they were associated with a white band. Do you know who Fletcher Henderson was?"

"A piano player."

"Yeah, and a band leader, too. He was the first black artist to play with an all white band. He joined Benny Goodman in the thirties. That's what made him famous."

"I guess the whole segregation issue was going on in this country at that time, huh?"

"As I said, a few made it. Satchmo made it, and Kid Ory made it, along with a handful of others. But most of the early day musicians had to find other jobs to keep from starvin'.'"

"How about you, Yawdy? Did you ever play with any big bands on a national basis?"

"Yep, when I was a young man, in the late forties and early fifties. I traveled a bit with my music."

"Did you enjoy it?"

"It's a tough life. As I said, black musicians were on a lower pay scale than the white guys. You can study musician after musician and see the difficulties from the lifestyle as well. I guess I just didn't want that for myself. So I decided to focus on my roots and paid attention to what I wanted to do: New Orleans jazz."

"But the swing era must have been hot at that time?"

"Mike, you gotta understand the power that started jazz has gone on to affect almost every type of music–gospel, ragtime, blues, swing, bee bop, R&B, reggae, and now even rap. Every type of music has come and gone from the forefront with the public. I was twenty-five in 1950. The big band and swing era was basically dead at that point."

"So you came back here?"

"Yes, and I'm glad I did. Now, we've been in here talkin' all this time and that new Gibson's just sittin' in there all by herself. Let's go hit the woodshed."

FOURTEEN

A Jazz Brunch

"What we play is life."

—Satchmo

The bright Sunday morning sunshine made my sport coat feel like a heated thermal blanket as I walked with Yawdy up river along Chartres. I'd driven to his house, but rather than drive back to the Hall, he preferred that we walk. It was 10:40 a.m. as we neared 726 Saint Peter Street. An old brown tweed clarinet case swung silently in Yawdy's right hand as we strolled along.

"You are walking pretty good today, Mr. Rum."

"Yes, indeed I am. Feelin' better, too."

"Amazing what a little medicine will do."

"Ah, maybe it was more from listenin' to that Gibson yesterday."

"Yawdy, if I was to spend a little more time pickin', and getting music lessons from you it'd be hard to tell what I might be able to do with that Gibson."

"Now wouldn't that just be somethin'," Yawdy added. "Goin' to be a lot of folks for you to meet today, Mister Mike."

"Will there be an audience?"

"No, not really, this is a private affair. We do a brunch at the Hall a couple, three times a year just for fun, usually just the musicians and some family."

When we got to the Hall, the wrought iron gate in the doorway was standing open a couple of feet. The old iron hinges moaned as Yawdy pushed back on the gate and stepped through.

"This here was the carriage way where the original owners parked their buggies," Yawdy explained.

"Did they board horses here as well?"

"I think mostly they were kept down the street at a livery stable."

A small gathering was assembled in the courtyard as we walked out of the carriage way. Sunlight filtered through the canopy of dogwood and pecan trees along with a single banana palm planted long ago in the courtyard. A round, wrinkled-faced lady immediately stepped up to us that I recognized as Ada Clark who had been the piano player I'd met on one of my first visits to the Hall.

"Good mornin', Yawdy Rum. We heard from your niece that you took a spell yesterday."

"Mornin', Ada. Ah, ain't nothin', I'm doin' fine now. You remember this fellow?"

Yawdy turned and grabbed my right elbow.

"Sure do, the salt guy. Sorry I couldn't make the gig on the *Creole Queen* other night."

"Everyone had a great time, Ms. Clark. They sure seemed to enjoy the jazz, that's for sure."

"Most everyone does. Makes a body happy."

Ada stood before us, beaming the brilliance of her life through the lines in her face. She wore a royal blue cotton dress with a luminescent string of pearls down the front. I felt the warmth in her palm and fingers as we shook hands, and then continued to remain in the grip for an extended moment.

"That's a very attractive dress you are wearing this morning, Ms. Clark," I said.

"Well, ain't you a sweet one. I figured even if I wasn't goin' to the Lord's house today, I'd still dress up a bit for all these old coots. Yawdy, there all kinds of good eats upstairs."

"Thanks, Ada, we'll head up a little later."

Several members of the band were beginning to assemble themselves on an assortment of old wooden and metal folding chairs lining the far wall of the courtyard. Yawdy took time to make sure I was introduced to everyone. Each of the band members whom I'd met on my earlier visit to the Hall were there—Zeb on the trumpet, Cosmo on trombone, Mash on the banjo, Gigi on the bass, and Emmett on drums. As with an earlier night in the Hall, each was wearing dark slacks, a white dress shirt, and what had to be a favorite necktie. The group's ties displayed a various array of stripes, plaids, and polka dots. Yawdy's tie was shiny gold with different sizes of black polka dots running the full length of it. He tied it a bit short so it ended about two inches above his belt. Each band member had one or more family members with them in the courtyard. The south Louisiana patois was like a cacophony from the assembled family and musicians.

"Ms. Clark, it looks like we are missing your piano." I remarked.

"We don't move that ol' rattle trap of a piano out of the Hall. It would plum fall to pieces rollin' out here on the bricks. So, if'n it's okay with you, I'll just tap my foot this mornin'."

She raised her dress high enough to display an elastic band pulled up just below her right knee. It was ringed with jingle bells.

"I got these to help the ol' mens stay in time. Always works too." She laughed a good belly laugh that resonated deep within her as she let her dress fall back to her mid-calf. Yawdy picked up a mute that was sitting on the chair next to Cosmo and stuck it in his horn.

"Mister Mike, sometimes we got to tone down ol' Cosmo a bit. He's 'bout half b-flat and mostly saliva; keeps us dry if he uses the mute."

"Yawdy, you old bum. You wouldn't know what a b-flat was if'n it hit you up side the head," Cosmo spouted back.

I stood there watching the friendly bantering go back and forth. They were all fair game to each other. They say you measure the worth of a person by the number of friends they have. That being the case, Yawdy was indeed a very rich man. Yawdy took his clarinet from the case, assembled the sections, and began soaking the reed in his mouth. He asked me to place the case in the carriage way for safekeeping. I stepped around the corner to place it in the cool shade just inside the doorway. When I did, I bumped into a figure I hadn't seen in the shadows. I was surprised. It was Adrian, the shopkeeper from Reverend Zombie's shop across the street.

"Excuse me. I didn't see you."

"Oh, no problem, are they getting ready to play?" she asked.

"I think so. It looks like everyone is gathering around. It sure feels like a family affair."

"Well, that's all they are, just family to each other."

"Family folk who really know their music," I added. "What are you doing on this side of the street?"

"Hey, I'm always up for a bit of fun. Do you still have that charm I sold you?"

"Got it right here," I reached into the pocket of my slacks and pulled out the silver guitar charm I had purchased from her a when I was in New Orleans back in August. "You said it was good luck."

"How is it working?"

"I'd say I'm lucky to be here today getting to listen to these guys."

We heard Yawdy counting off behind us. "A one, a two, a one, two, three, four…."

"Come on, let's grab a seat," she said.

It was one song after another all morning. They took a minute to introduce, and tell a story about each one, just a little background to help everyone connect with the song. They played "Basin Street," "Indian Love Call," "Liza Jane," "Eh la bas," "The Saint Louis Blues," "Down by the Riverside," "The Saint James Infirmary," "Oh! Didn't It Rain," and on and on. Adrian seemed to know them all and could sing out right along with the band. They even played a New Orleans rendition of "Just a Closer Walk with Thee" to close out the Sunday morning set. When they finally broke up, Yawdy made it over to where I was sitting. Adrian had left a few minutes earlier. She said she was going to help with the food.

"Come on, Mister Mike, let's go upstairs and grab a bite to eat."

I followed Yawdy through a large wooden door at the edge of the carriage way and up a flight of well-worn stairs. My hand slid along the soft bare wood banister railing as we climbed the steps. A row of lightly frosted single-pane windows ran along the second story of the up river side of the building. We stepped onto the landing at the top of the stairway and into a makeshift kitchen.

"We always keep a little somethin' for a body to eat up here, but I think you'll find about anythin' you can imagine today," Yawdy explained.

Four card tables, offering a smorgasbord of home cooked delicacies and filled to the point of collapse, greeted us a few steps from the top of the stairway. Fresh carrots, radishes and pickled okra, along with a half dozen assorted Tupperware bowls of mixed fruit salads covered the first table. Some of the salads even had fresh puffy marshmallows mixed in. There were homemade rolls and hot corn fritters, mufaletta sandwiches, red beans and rice, and more different kinds of fried stuff than I'd ever seen in one place. My mouth watered before I even started to fill my plate. Yawdy pointed to what looked like sliced turkey of some sort but without any bones.

"You gotta get some of this. You ever had a turducken?" he asked.

"A what?"

"A Turducken, mmmm mmm. You take an old gobblin' turkey, stuff him with a big fat duck, then stuff the duck with a chicken, coat it with a special hot seasonin' rub, and bake it till it's golden brown—turducken!"

I was trying to balance my plate and hold on to a glass of sweet tea, when I bumped into Adrian again.

"Well, excuse me one more time."

"That's okay, there's not a lot of room up here with all this food."

She stepped around me and kissed Yawdy on the cheek. "Hi, Uncle Yawdy, how are you feeling today?"

"Just fine, Adrian. Let me introduce you to a friend of mine. Mister Mike, this is my niece, Adrian. Adrian, this is Mike; he's a pal of mine from Minnesota."

I know I had to look surprised as we made eye contact. "I didn't know you were...you never said you were..."

"Yawdy's niece," she offered.

"Well, yes."

"Well, you never asked."

"Yawdy, we've met. She's quite a salesperson and a historian, too."

"Yeah, she takes care of me as well," Yawdy added.

"Uncle Yawdy, am I going to have to come over and hand feed those pills to you or are you going to behave?"

"Oh, I'm gonna take 'em. I'm already feelin' better today."

"Yeah, you old toot. You get to feelin' better and then you fall off the wagon."

"Nah, I promised you. I'll do my part," he said as he winked at her with his left eye.

After everyone had eaten, the band got together for one more set, then folks started clearing out. I walked back through the carriage way, and stepped up into the main performance hall in the front portion of the building. The only light was from the cracks between the hurricane shutters in place across the front windows. Fine dust particles floated in the two thin beams of light entering the room. Champ arose from the cushion on the piano bench and gave me a raspy meow. There was as much cat hair on the piano cushion as on the old cat himself. "Hi, fella. What do you say, pretty comfortable in here, huh?"

What a historic place. How many musicians had performed here? I closed my eyes, took a deep breath, and inhaled the musty smell of wood and dried sweat. It was the smell of life, of humanity. The fragrance of people coming together to experience all it means to be human. I opened my eyes and looked down at the old cat rubbing against my pants.

The old upright piano stood silently to my right. The piano keys were cracked, yellowed, and a few of the ivories were missing altogether. The varnish on the aging instrument had long since weathered from the years in the Hall. I reached out and laid my hand on top of the piano. The old cracked surface felt dry and rough to my touch.

"Gives you goose bumps, doesn't it?"

I heard Yawdy's voice behind me in the doorway. I didn't turn around. I just stood in the dimly lit room.

"Yawdy, you love this place."

"I should say."

"But you love it for more than the building. You love it for the fellowship, for the music, for those who have come before you."

"Mmmm hmm, that I do."

"Yawdy, we've talked a lot about the need for a person to find their passion and to have the confidence to set out on a plan to achieve their goals and dreams. You said you had a secret."

"Yep."

"Does it deal with how to achieve your goals?"

"Could be and more too."

"More?"

"Yeah, like how to harmonize every aspect of your life."

"And it is?"

"What, the secret?"

"Yes."

"It's somethin' you already know."

FIFTEEN

Beignets and Chicory

*"Jazz opposes to our classical conception of music
a strange and subversive chaos of sounds.
It is a fashion, and as such, destined someday to disappear."*

—Igor Stravinsky

We stepped through the gate and out onto the sidewalk in front of the Hall.

"Yawdy, do you want to walk back to your place, or do you want to catch a cab?"

"I prefer walkin', if you can keep up with me. You were kind of sluffin' it on the way over this morning."

Yawdy took off down the sidewalk at a good pace.

"Hey, I was up early and got in almost five miles this morning. What'd you do?"

"I got up, went to the bathroom. That was a good thing. I think anybody that'd go run five miles is nuts."

"Yawdy, what's the background story on the Hall?"

"You mean the buildin', the name, or the music?"

"Adrian gave me the history of the building. I'm asking more about how it came to be a music hall."

"Larry Borenstein. Now, there was some cat!"

"He started it?"

"Round-a-bout. Ol' Larry had an art gallery at 726 Saint Peter. Don't know if he ever made any money runnin' it. More of a property guy here in the Quarter than anythin'. He was always a buyin' and sellin' stuff.

"So what was the Hall, a hangout or where he lived?"

"It was his art gallery and, on occasion, he'd have some musicians come in and play just to bring in some foot traffic. He'd always made sure someone passed the hat for us. Zeb and I was playin' one time with some guys from the navy base back in the late fifties and someone turned us in to the police."

"Turned you in, for what?"

"Well, a couple of those guys were white, and there used to be a law against folks of a different color playin' together. One fellow we played with was a cornet player from up your way named Charlie DeVore. Darn good one, too. Charlie knew so much about traditional jazz we called him the walkin' encyclopedia of jazz. Ol' Larry ended up bailin' us all out of the precinct jail back o' town on Rampart. Larry was a little rough on the outside, but on the inside he was all good."

"So did he change it from an art gallery to a music hall?"

"He ended up leasin' the Hall to a guy named Mills. He and a real nice lady named Barbara Reid got it goin'. But Larry didn't like the way they was doin' things."

"So what happened?"

"Mills and Barbara set up a non-profit jazz society. I think ol' Larry was lookin' out for us musicians and wanted the Hall to be a for-profit venture."

"So he took it back over?"

"Nope. Raised the rent so high they couldn't afford the place, so they shut down. Day or so later a fella named Alan Jaffe opened it back up."

"What was Jaffe's connection?"

"He was a tuba player and someone ol' Larry liked."

"Where did the name for the place come from?"

"Mills and Barbara thought it up and it stuck."

"It's a great name."

"Well, some folks didn't like thinkin' about preservin' anythin'. Shoot, we were just lookin' for a place to play, and hopin' we could keep our music alive. Some of us kinda liked Authenticy Hall."

"But the name Preservation Hall stuck."

"Sure did. I think Alan and Miz Sandy liked it, so they kept it. Let's step across the street, and I'll show you a little somethin'."

We crossed Chartres Street in front of the old white marble Saint Louis Cathedral and into Jackson Square. I followed Yawdy across the grass into the center of the square where he stopped in front of a magnificent bronze statue of General Andrew Jackson aglow in the midday Crescent City sun.

"Mister Mike, did you ever hear the statement that fame favors the bold?"

"If I did, I don't recall it."

"Well, there are two examples right here."

"Now, take ol' General Jackson. He gave the British a whippin' in the battle of New Orleans. He took a chance and included some four hundred free blacks to help him. They killed two thousand British and only suffered a small number of casualties. It made him famous and probably ended up puttin' him in the White House."

"So that's the reason for his statue here?"

"Uh-huh now, if you'll notice, ol' Jackson is tippin' his hat. There was a lady named Baroness Micaela Pontabella. She lived on the east side of the square. She got married, and moved to France when she was fifteen. Her father-in-law must have been some kind of nut 'cause he tried to kill her."

"Why was that?"

"Don't know if I ever heard, but rumor has it he shot off two of her fingers in the process. She came back to New Orleans and was instrumental in the development of the city and on preservin' green space."

"Pretty precious commodity in a low lying area like New Orleans," I added.

"You bet. And now look what we get to enjoy thanks to her."

"So, Yawdy, is the secret you've hinted that fame favors those who do bold things?"

"Nope. Just wanted to show what happens when people put their mind to somethin'. It's amazin' what a little focus can do."

I felt like I was pulling teeth. The old man was leading me around, showing me things, explaining the roots of jazz, parks, and city squares, and yet remaining somewhat elusive. I recalled he mentioned a secret the day we were in Louis Armstrong Park. What was it and did it have anything to do with me? Was he searching for something in me that would let him know it was okay to share his secret with me? The questions in my mind were penetrating.

"Come on, Mister Mike. I could use a cup of coffee, how about you?"

Yawdy headed across the square with me in tow. We walked across Decatur to Café Du Monde. The smell of fresh baked bread had my taste buds quivering before we had even walked in the door.

"Beignets," I said.

Yawdy's eyebrows formed two raised crescents on his forehead and his pink tongue encircled his lips as he said, "A body can't walk by the Square and not stop for a cup of joe and nibble on a beignet."

He led me to a seat next to the windows facing Decatur Street. The wide green and white striped wallpaper above the kitchen reflected off the shaded windows. Yawdy slid his clarinet case underneath the table between us.

A tiny-framed, middle-aged Asian waitress greeted us with a slight nod of her head and little more than a smile.

"Mister Mike, are you up for a little bite of somethin'?"

"You march me into a place smells like my grandma's kitchen, and then you ask me that question. Why, absolutely, Mr. Rum."

Yawdy looked eye level at the waitress who was patiently anticipating our decision.

"Two black coffees and a single order, please, ma'am."

"Yes, sir, Mr. Yawdy, we'll get that right up for you," she replied.

"I think everyone knows you in this town, Yawdy."

"Pert' near. Maybe I ought to think about runnin' for mayor, ha."

"Hey, don't laugh. You never know."

"We never did get around to talkin' 'bout the salt business yesterday. How's it goin' for you?" he asked.

"About the same, maybe even a bit more tenuous."

"How's that?"

"Well, I think there is a career myth that many of us in the business world live by. That working your way up the ladder is a good thing. Taking on more and more responsibility is what you are supposed to do."

"And you don't think movin' up is a good thing?"

"Maybe for some, but I'm not sure for me."

"Why not?"

"Yawdy, don't take this wrong because I've really enjoyed getting to know you and have the opportunity to spend time with you."

"Likewise."

"I've been on the road almost four days a week for the past seven weeks. This trip, I'm away from home ten days straight. My kids have grown up and in some ways I don't feel I really know them. I'd like to spend some more time with my wife as I get older, not less because my job requires so much of my time."

"Mister Mike, why don't you get after writin' that book that's inside of you?"

"I suppose time. The last thing I want to do at the end of the day is spend more time on a computer. Everyone has to have a little downtime. That's why I love my music so much. It's a total escape from my daily routine."

"So besides time, what's holdin' you back?"

"I imagine the golden handcuffs."

"Golden handcuffs. What do you mean?"

"When you become an officer in a major corporation, your compensation gets to be much more involved than just your salary."

"Like what?"

"Stock options, long-term compensation, special insurance benefits, and the like."

"I wouldn't know nothin' about that kinda stuff."

"If I walk away from the business now, I forfeit a substantial sum."

"Life ain't all about money," Yawdy added.

"I know that."

"Got any savin's that'd get you by for a while?"

"Yes."

"How long?"

"I'm not sure."

"Well, you gotta find out. Then you'd know what you can do."

Our waitress brought the steaming chicory coffee and fresh beignets and sat them on the table. They were four of the most beautiful, golden nuggets of dough–snowcapped mountains with glistening white powdered sugar I'd ever seen. The sweet aroma from the beignets wafted above the table.

Yawdy continued, "Beignets, the cook takes little dollops of dough, and drops 'em in a deep fryer. When they come out, they get sprinkled with powdered sugar. I'll split 'em with you."

Split them with me, heck, if I had wasted any time, ol' Yawdy would have inhaled those sweet dollops of fresh deep fried indulgence. The powdered sugar stuck to every finger, and I didn't want to miss a lick. The vapor off the steaming cups of chicory circled between us at the table. There's just something about Du Monde's chicory coffee–dark, full-flavored, and an aroma that tells me this is the best coffee shop in the world.

"So, Mister Mike, what do you want more: money and the prestige of that job you got or to take life and do what you want to with it?"

I agreed that was the core question.

Yawdy continued, "Sounds like to me you have some thinkin' to do. Thinkin' about what you want to do and then decidin' to do somethin' about it. I'm hearin' you say you ain't really got a choice. If you stay where you are, you gotta continue to make sacrifices. If you stay where you are, you gotta conform to their expectations. And if you stay where you are, you can't accomplish your personal goals."

I licked my lips to recover every drop of the snowy powdered sugar left from each bite of the beignets. As I did, I began feeling the same way about what Yawdy was trying to tell me. What he was saying was important, and I didn't want to miss a word. Yawdy was on a roll. He kept after me.

"Mister Mike, if the slaves in New Orleans wouldn't have looked for the joy in their souls, we might not have jazz. If General Jackson hadn't reached out to the slaves for help, he might have not whipped the British. If the baroness wouldn't have come back to New Orleans, there might not be a Jackson Square. Are you familiar with the musical term, 'D.C. al Fine'?"

"Why sure, D.C. means dal capo, the head, and al Fine, the end. It means to play from the beginning of a piece of music to the end."

Yawdy nodded his head in agreement, and then said, "Ol' Yawdy has another meanin' for it. I've told you there're lots of applications from the world of music for our lives. D.C. al Fine is one of those tools. If you'll go back to the beginnin' in your mind, the beginnin' of whatever goal you are tryin' to work on, and think it through to the end, you'll find all kinds of motivation within you for action. It'll clarify your thinkin'. It'll give you perspective. Go back to the beginnin', and think it through all the way to a successful outcome. When you take time to think things through, you gain insight. Maybe that's how ol' General Jackson figured out how to whip the British. Maybe, that's how the baroness figured out how to make it back to New Orleans. Maybe that's how ol' Mister Mike will figure out if he really has the fire in his belly to do what he wants to with the rest of his life. Do you know who Ferdinand Magellan was?"

"Sure. He was an early explorer."

"Do you know what he said?"

"No. I don't think so."

"He said the sea was a dangerous place and its storms terrible, but those obstacles have never been sufficient to cause a person to remain ashore."

"So that's the secret. I need to go back to the beginning in my mind, review what I want to do and press on regardless of the obstacles."

"That'n more."

SIXTEEN

The Hogan Archives

"Jazz has always been a man telling the truth about himself."

—Quincy Jones

A little over five months had transpired since my conversation with Yawdy at Café Du Monde that Sunday in New Orleans. The questions he posed to me that day had been my constant companions since our last time together. A week or so earlier I learned I needed to make a trip to New Orleans, so I'd called Yawdy to make sure we could get together. He asked me if I'd ever been to the Hogan Jazz Archives. When I told him no, he said it was a place we needed to visit the next time I came to town.

Yawdy and I walked from Freret Street across the campus of Tulane University to the Howard-Tilton Memorial Library. A stiff breeze tugged at Yawdy's black beret as we walked along. All of a sudden he took off singing lightly.

"Everyday I'm a walkin' with the King, walkin' with the King, walkin' with the King. Sing haleluuuuuia, I'm a walkin' with the King. That devil, he's a tryin' to get me but I'm a walkin' with the King."

"What prompted that?" I asked.

"The ol' devil. He's livin' in my feet."

"Have you been doing the foot stretches I showed you?"

"Some of 'em. Say, what's the temperature up your way these days?" Yawdy asked.

"Not too bad. Mostly in the high twenties the last week or so, but we've still got about a foot of snow on the ground. It's about usual for March in Minnesota."

"My old bones wouldn't take kindly to that."

"You just have to dress for it."

"Well, I ain't got that many duds. Ol' Mash was with the tourin' band back in the sixties. I think it was February or March and they were up your way. He said it was so cold, he wore a stockin' hat day and night just to keep his ol' cue ball warm."

"Minnesota winters can be chilly."

"Here, Mister Mike, we go in right here."

"I thought we were headed for the library."

"It's across from here. The Hogan Jazz Archives are in Jones Hall."

"What's all here?"

"Everythin' that means anythin' when it comes to jazz—oral histories, recorded music, sheet music, photographs, orchestrations, all kinds of manuscripts, and clippins'."

"Anything about you in here?"

"Now you just never know, do you?"

At least I felt I had a line on his so-called secret. I had come to the conclusion that Yawdy believed the most important thing for a person to do was to take a look at life and not be afraid to make a change. We walked up to a dark skinned, handsome young man of about twenty wearing thick black horn-rim glasses and working at a desk near the entry to the archives. As we stepped up, he wriggled his nose to straighten his glasses.

"Good evening, Mister Yawdy. In for a little peek at something?"

"When did you start workin' the desk, Alexander?"

"I've been working here at night all semester."

"That's why we haven't seen you at the Hall."

"Yes, sir."

Yawdy turned and tugged on my jacket sleeve. "Mister Mike, Alexander's granddaddy, Mister Percy Humphrey, played with the Hall for many years. In fact, he led the tourin' band for most of that time."

"Hello, Alexander. It's nice to meet you. Are you a musician, too?"

"I aim to be. There is a long history of the affliction in our family."

"I think that's a good thing." He nodded his head in agreement.

Yawdy leaned over the counter and said, "I figured some sweet young miss latched on to those curly locks of yours and was holdin' you down somewhere."

"No, sir, Mister Yawdy, I've been studying hard."

"Well, don't stay away too long, you might learn somethin' from us down at the Hall. Of course might not be anythin' you could use, but you'd learn it nonetheless."

Yawdy pushed himself back from the counter and swung around to my right. He seemed to know exactly where he was headed. Yawdy picked up an array of books as we strolled through the library. It appeared he had a number of special volumes, knew where each one was located, and could pull them off the shelf without even looking at the titles. We sat down next to each other at a long heavy walnut conference table in a small clearing amid the volumes of books and materials. He showed me volume after volume containing pictures of many of the early New Orleans jazz artists. He had a humorous story or anecdote to go along with each one.

"You see this picture, Mister Mike?" He pointed to a black and white photo of a thin-faced older black bass player in the customary white dress shirt with black suspenders.

"Sure, the bass player?"

"His name was Papa John Joseph. He was born near here in Saint James Parish about the same year as Buddy Bolden. 'Member me talkin' about Bolden?"

"Yep."

Yawdy turned the page. There was a photo of Yawdy and Papa John standing in front of Preservation Hall. Both were holding big fat cigars.

"Yawdy, I didn't know you smoked."

"Oh, I haven't smoked for years, but when I did, let me tell you, man, I got after 'em."

"Just cigars?"

"Nope, cigarettes too, and lots of 'em. Seemed like everybody used to smoke. It was just the thing to do."

"How'd you quit?"

"It was tougher'n hell, but I finally did it. They say nicotine is more addictive than heroin. Darn, if I don't believe 'em."

"So how'd you do it?"

"I guess I finally started payin' attention to the effect they were havin' on my ability to play my instrument. I tried everythin' I could find to quit. I listened to tapes, got hypnotized, tried acupuncture, and even voodoo."

"What did it?"

"Got re-programmed."

"Re-programmed?"

"Yep. One day I saw this ad in the *Times-Picayune* on a session that was bein' held at the Marquette Hotel. So I called 'em up and told 'em I wanted to attend."

"What did it amount to?"

"Basically, this fella who led the class talked all about the health aspects of smokin'. He had us go buy a pack of filtered cigarettes at the break and come back to the room. Then he made us tear off the filters and over the course of an hour or so we smoked about half of 'em. Reminded me of smokin' roll-your-owns, only worse."

"You quit by smoking?"

"Yep. He'd have us hold in a puff until we was turnin' blue, coughin', and about to die. While we was doin' that, he'd talk about what that smoke was doin' to our lungs. Then when we was about to pass out, damn if he wouldn't have us take in another puff, and hold it in again."

"Didn't it make you sick?" I asked.

"Sicker 'n a dead man. That same night ol' Papa John was playin' with us. We'd just finished us a rip roarin' round of 'When the Saints Go Marchin' In', and I heard ol' Papa John behind me say, 'damn, that piece about did me in.' Then he just collapsed, and died right there in the Hall."

"Heart attack?"

"I think so."

"Was he a heavy smoker?"

"Yep. He certainly had his share of 'em."

"So was it the class or his death that caused you to quit?"

"Both. And because I finally started payin' attention to what they were doin' to me. I didn't want to end up like ol' Papa John. When you get serious about somethin' and you focus on it, you can change."

"So, you quit cold turkey."

"Stone cold. Tough, too. Every time after that when I wanted one, I just thought about the things that fellow had said in that class, about how bad I felt, and ol' Papa layin' there on the floor. I never lit up another one."

"Yawdy, why do you think it is so hard for us to see the negative self-destructive things we do to ourselves?"

"Probably because it all comes on us so slow we don't realize it until we're trapped by our actions and habits. Even then, if'n a person don't stop and give some thought to what's goin' on in their lives, they may never see it until it's too late."

"I guess recognizing the problem is one thing and finding the courage to make a change is another."

"Well, if I had a kept smokin', I might have had to give up my life like ol' Papa John. I'm sayin' you have to make a trade-off to get somethin' you want. That's how it's always been for me. If you want to accomplish somethin' in your life, you gotta give up the time on other things to do it. If you are carryin' too much weight, you gotta learn to give up some grub and get a little exercise. Same for smokin' or drinkin' or chasin'. You can't have a happy marriage and be runnin' around. You gotta make a commitment and stick to it."

Yawdy reached across the table and picked up one of the last books he had pulled from the shelves. He opened the cover and flipped about halfway through the pages before he laid it on the table in front of us. It was a picture of Yawdy standing next to Louis Armstrong in front of Carnegie Hall in New York City.

"I wondered if you knew him."

"Oh, yeah, ol' Satchmo was a dear friend."

"Did you know him through the Hall?"

"Yep, and as a kid, too."

"How's that?"

"He was friends with my dad. After my dad died, Louis would often stop by when he was in New Orleans to check on my mom. He'd even play the horn for my uncle Benny."

"That had to be something."

"Oh, it was. He was bigger'n life."

"What's the story behind the picture?"

"It was 1947, I was twenty-two years old, and I had been travelin' on and off for about a year as a backup on the sax with Satchmo's band."

"You mean like second chair?"

"Kinda. I didn't play with Louis on stage every bookin'. We was in New York and his manager, Joe Glazer, convinced him that folks wanted a more traditional small combo versus a bigger band."

"Wow, Yawdy, you were set to play a gig with Louis Armstrong at Carnegie Hall in New York City!"

"That was the original plan, but Joe convinced him otherwise. I think Satchmo felt bad for puttin' us cats out of the grub line."

"That's a bummer."

"Not at all, Mister Mike. That was a blessin' in disguise for me."

"How's that?"

"It's a mighty tough life for a travelin' jazz musician. Long days, late nights, lots of drinkin', and even drugs. If you study anythin' about the jazz world, you'll find a trail of broken lives everywhere you turn."

"So the change in the band was an out for you?"

"Yeah, man. I hot-footed it back to New Orleans and made my life here."

"And got married?"

"Uh-huh."

"But she died."

"Yeah, but my life has always been right here. This is where I feel happiest."

"But didn't you tell me you traveled on and off with the Preservation Hall band over the years?"

"Oh, I toured for the Hall, but that was different. We had the Jaffes helping to make it somethin' special. We stuck to our roots, and we always came back here."

"Like family?"

"Uh-huh. We all supported each other—playin', laughin', fightin', and prayin'."

"But what an experience getting to play with Louis Armstrong."

"Oh, what you talkin' 'bout; it was worth a million bucks."

"What do you remember the most?"

"You mean about him as a person or what he taught me?"

"Both."

"Well, from a musical standpoint, Satchmo had extreme concentration. He could take one single note and play it for eight bars. Any other musician tries that, and the audience would get up and walk out. He used to say to me, 'Yawdy, take that note, bend it, squeak it, growl it, whine it, cry it, bark it, and make it sing'."

"So he played one note but in many variations."

"You got it. The devil's in the details."

"And how was he as a person?"

"I don't know if I can really separate the man from the music. He used to say his whole life, his whole spirit, was to blow that horn. I guess I'd say he had lots of *hokum*."

"Hokum?"

"What, you never heard that word before?"

"I don't think so."

"Satchmo had a great sense of humor. Hokum means fun. Hokum means wild, kinda zaney stuff. New Orleans jazz has always contained a certain amount of hokum. The Satchmo I knew was a happy man."

"Yawdy, I think you are a happy man."

"Mister Mike, I got some gumbo and cold beer in my fridge. A little right now would make me a happy man, how about you?"

"Lead the way, Mr. Rum."

SEVENTEEN

Humbug Jitters

"True jazz is an art of individual assertion within and against the group."

—Ralph Ellison

The soft glow of the light from inside the fridge enveloped Yawdy's face when he opened the door, pulled out a large brown plastic Tupperware bowl and two icy bottles of beer.

"Here, Mister Mike, if you'll open these, I'll get the gumbo in the pot."

"Where's your opener, Yawdy?"

"Take a look in that skinny little drawer on the right side of the sink."

I wiped back the cold beads of sweat from the label on the beer bottle. "Acadian Pilsner, where do you get this?"

"It comes from a local brewery here in the Crescent City. They don't make a lot of it. Believe most of it gets sold around here."

Yawdy removed a large cast iron kettle from under the cabinet and spooned the gumbo into the midnight black pot.

"A little gumbo, a little rice, some spiced apple rings, and some soda crackers. That work for you?"

"It sounds good to me. What's in the gumbo?"

"Now, ol' Yawdy don't give out his secrets to just anybody. Do you cook?"

"Love to. On weekends my wife and I crack open a bottle of wine and make a big mess in the kitchen together. Home cooking is a bit of heaven when you spend as much time on the road as I do."

The Tupperware let out a whishing sound as Yawdy popped open the lid of the gumbo. "This here's a chicken and crab gumbo. There's a fella I know named Gottsche, works in the oil patch down at Venice. He lives over at Ocean Springs, Mississippi. You know where that is?"

"Yep, just east of Gulfport."

"Well, he's one heck of fisherman. I don't know where he gets all 'em blue crabs, but he keeps me stocked up. He's even got a key to my place and leaves me all kinds of surprises in the ice box. You ever hear of King and Cobia?"

"Is that a song or a jazz band?"

"Na, they're fish, man. King Mackerel and Cobia. They migrate along the Gulf, all the way down to the Keys. Mmmm mmm. Now, let me tell you, when he leaves me a big ol' package of Cobia, do I ever eat good."

Yawdy's kitchen was a comfortable place. Messy enough to tell that someone lived there and as aromatic as a Louisiana spice house. The braided rug at the sink was tattered but fully functional. Several of the cabinets didn't quite close all the way, and there were more than enough fingerprints to tell the aging kitchen was well-used. I found the opener in the drawer, uncapped both bottles, and handed one to Yawdy.

"Here you go, Mr. Rum. Good to be with you." Yawdy took the bottle and tipped it towards mine in a toast.

"Same here. You got the new worn off of that Gibson yet?"

"Hardly. I've only traveled with it one time, the last time I was down here. Mostly, I still pick on the Alvarez when I'm on the road."

"Nothin' wrong with the way it sounds."

Yawdy pulled an old glass canister out from underneath the cabinet. He removed the lid and measured out a cup of brown rice into a waiting pan of water he'd already placed on the stove next to the gumbo. He stood on his tiptoes and grabbed some cobalt blue Fiestaware from the cabinet.

He handed the plates to me and said, "Here, make yourself useful and clean us off a spot to have dinner."

A three or four day supply of the *Times-Picayune* lay scattered about the table along with an old black-handled pair of scissors and some clippings Yawdy had cut from the papers. The word Dixieland appeared across the top of one article he had cut out. I stacked the items neatly at the end of the table to provide room for our dinner.

"Yawdy, you always use the term, New Orleans jazz, for the style of music you play. How does what you play compare to Dixieland jazz?"

He continued to stir the gumbo, scrunched up one cheek, and appeared to ponder a response.

"I'd say Dixieland was more of a social or racial distinction than a musical one. Do you know who Al Hirt was?"

"Yeah, a trumpet player. I think my mom had all of his albums. I used to listen to them when I was a kid."

"We called him the big, round mound of sound. Man, that cat could play. Ol' Al was a trained musician from a classical sense. His technique was excellent. Take a tune like, 'Tin Roof Blues,' man, he could blow the bell off. But, at the end of the day ol' Al was a white guy. Nothin' against him mind you, but his version of traditional New Orleans jazz, well, that's what I'd call Dixieland. There is just a difference in the rhythm. I would add one thing, though."

"What's that?"

"Al was a great guy. He was a very generous man and helped a lot of aspiring musicians along the path. Ol' Al loved New Orleans and spent his whole life in and out of here. Lots of other musicians claimed to be from New Orleans, but never really spent any time here. Al passed away a few years ago. I don't think he's ever been given the due he deserves for supportin' the Crescent City and, more importantly, jazz."

"Yawdy, what do you think makes New Orleans jazz so appealing to folks the world over?"

"Lots of things."

"Like what? What is there about it that really connects with people?"

"Well, now it don't connect with everybody. Shoot, if it did, ol' Yawdy would be a millionaire."

"Okay," I agreed, "maybe not everyone, but you have to admit that it certainly has a dedicated following."

"Mister Mike, I think folks like excitement. I think they want to feel like they share in some way with the musician."

"But you're not talking about singing?"

"No. I'm talkin' about harmony, improvisation, and spontaneity. African music was all about that–work songs, love songs, funeral songs, and the like. The original jazz in one form or another was all about that. I think folks can relate to traditional jazz 'cause it's a reflection of life."

The air in the kitchen began to fill with the pungent zing of the gumbo. Yawdy opened a pint-sized mason jar of cherry-red spiced apple rings, placed them on the table, and sat down in the chair across the corner of the table from me.

"Yawdy, I could make a comparison between business and jazz."

"How's that?" he asked.

"Well, some employees are more spontaneous than others, more likely to go against the flow or challenge the direction in which the business is moving."

"Uh-huh."

"Some managers have hell of a time with that."

"You back to talkin' about fittin' into someone else's expectations?" he asked.

"Right. When a jazz musician takes off on an improvisational riff, you never really know where they're going, or exactly when they'll come back."

"Well, I got a general idea how long the riff might last. A riff might go thirty-two bars, or it might be a night when the other guy is really hot, and he might go sixty-four. Experience helps you with the timing of things, especially when you played a piece a thousand times. But, that's what jazz is all about."

I looked past Yawdy to the stove just in time to see the rice pot erupt into a foaming volcano. Yawdy tried to stand up quickly to get it, but his foot grabbed him, and the wrinkles on his forehead tightened as he sat back down in the chair.

I jumped up, put my hand on his right shoulder, and said, "Sit right there, I'll get it." I turned the flame down on the burner and wiped up the sticky spill with an old yellow dishrag I found lying over the center of the sink. "How are you doing on beer?" I asked.

"I'm good, but help yourself to another one if you'd like. I got plenty."

I grabbed another icy bottle from the fridge, popped the cap, and sat back down at the shiny chrome art deco table with my aging friend.

"Where were we?" I asked.

"I think you were sayin' improvisation was a good thing."

"Oh, yeah. I'm saying that the total outcome is better because you allow everyone to express their individuality."

"Mister Mike, jazz, to varin' degrees, allows the musician to be both within and against the group. But it's not a free-for-all. There are conventions to follow. Take New Orleans jazz for instance. There's room for the individual performer to strut and share that struttin' with his or her fellow band members. Now, if you look at hot jazz, bop, or even cool jazz, it is much more about improvisation than what I've spent most of my life playin'. Heck, there's times on some of the new stuff I plum lose the melody."

"I'm not sure I follow you."

"Why, we were talkin' about the master this afternoon at the library."

"Louis Armstrong?"

"Yeah, man. Ol' Satchmo turned the jazz world on its ear. More than any other performer, he changed jazz by bringin' the contribution of the individual artist to the forefront. He was a stylist."

"Okay, Yawdy, back to business. I think, for whatever reason, the corporate world has a hard time with improvisation."

"Probably scares 'em," he added.

"They want things predictable. Oh, they talk a good story about giving people room to explore and grow and try and fail, but they tolerate it only to a certain point."

"Mister Mike, if you'd be so kind, I'll take that second beer."

The old refrigerator opened with barely the touch of a finger. I reached in and retrieved another bottle of the delicious New Orleans brew. I wiped the sweat from the outside of the bottle with a paper towel, popped the cap, and handed the cold beer to Yawdy.

"Window dressin'," Yawdy added. "Someone comes along that's a free spirit, steps out a bit, and makes 'em nervous."

Yawdy reached over and gave my left arm a light squeeze. "But, you gotta remember that an orchestra has to have a score for the musicians to follow. Otherwise, you'd have a free-for-all, the bigger the organization, the bigger the need for a common score."

"Okay, Yawdy, there can be rules, but there should be room for flexibility at the same time."

The metal frame of his chair squeaked a bit as he leaned back away from the table.

"Mister Mike, I'd say some band leaders deal with it better than others. In fact, we used to get in a hell of a humbug over some songs."

"What's humbug?" I asked, not sure I heard the term correctly.

"Squabblin', bickerin', sometimes more—sometimes a down-and-out fight. One time on tour in Japan we had a couple of the band members start throwin' bottles of sake at each other."

"What'd you do?"

"We stopped playin' the songs they was fightin' over. That was better than gettin' rid of good musicians. Mister Mike, are you in the middle of some humbug in the salt business?"

"Yawdy, I think so. And I think it's heating up."

"Just a minute, I gotta turn up the heat on that gumbo or it ain't gonna be like I like it."

The hue of the gas flame changed from orange to bright blue as Yawdy turned up the heat, and then left the room to make a bathroom stop. While he was gone, I folded two thin, floral-printed paper towels for napkins, put out the silverware I found in a drawer, along with a miniature saxophone and clarinet salt and pepper set he'd placed on the end of the counter.

Yawdy returned to the kitchen from around the corner. "Doggone, I don't recall the last time I had two beers. I think I'm gonna be up all night, back and forth to the john. Here, in a bit you can open me another one, so I can make it worth my time. So what's the humbug?"

"Well, a while back there were several of us on a trip on the corporate jet to Utah with a couple of senior company officers."

"I thought that's what you were."

"Oh, no, there's a whole layer above me. All the division presidents report to the corporate chiefs. That's who these guys were. I report to one of the division guys."

Yawdy took a swig from his beer, sat the bottle down on the table, and replied, "So there was you, your boss, and the fat cats above him?"

"You got it. We had flown out to Salt Lake early in the morning, conducted a plant tour, and afterwards were holding a wrap-up session in the laboratory conference room at the plant. On the plant tour I had been asking lots of questions and offering some suggestions as usual."

"But aren't you on the sales end of things?"

"Yes. But I spent my earlier years working in both mine and plant operations. The two senior guys started playing stump the chump with me on some rather foolish operations questions."

"And what did you do?"

"Just tried to answer them and go on. So later that day we were on the corporate jet flying to Kansas for a dinner and these two guys are spouting off, bantering with everyone on board."

"But," Yawdy added insightfully, "I'll bet the humbug was really only comin' from one direction, from them."

"You got that right. These two bigwigs were like two sophomoric boys."

"So what happened?"

"So everyone's having a few cocktails, and I figure what the hell, let's all have some fun, not just the two ol' boys at the top."

"Here it comes," Yawdy said, as he began shaking his head back and forth.

"Well, I was sitting in a seat facing a guy named Harry. He was one of the chiefs who had asked me the trick questions earlier in the day at the plant. I decided to enter into a little friendly bantering back his direction. Nothing serious mind you. Just some friendly jabs."

"Mister Mike, you ol' dog. You messin' with fire with those cats. Their egos can't take it, especially from someone below 'em."

"Yawdy, I just figured if you were big enough to be picking on everyone else, then you ought to big enough to take a little picking yourself. So we went along for a few minutes exchanging some gentlemanly barbs until the air in the plane got so thick you could cut it with a knife. Ol' Harry's face turned as red as a pickled beet; that's when I knew he'd had enough. The newspaper he had been looking at earlier popped tight in his hands as he raised it up in front of his face and ended our conversation."

"How long ago was this?"

"Couple of weeks back," I answered.

"Heard anything since?"

"Nope."

"I'll bet you ain't out of the woods on this one. Kind'a like an ol' hurricane out there in the Gulf."

"Hurricane, how's that Yawdy?"

"They try to forecast when and where they are going to come on land, but they never know for sure till they hit. Them ol' hurricanes sit out there in the Gulf, in that warm water and they churn and build up steam. Then when they start movin', you gotta pay attention."

"Yawdy, you think my improvisation, my spontaneity, my orneriness has a hurricane headed my way?"

"I don't know, but what do you say we have some gumbo and split another one of them beers before it hits?"

EIGHTEEN
Late Night at Du Monde

"The pauses between the notes, ah,
that's where the art resides."

—Arthur Schnable

The attorneys for the firm operating at Port Fourchon had requested an emergency project review meeting. Control of the brine barges in the event of a direct hit by a Gulf hurricane had become a nagging issue. Considering it was mid May, we still had plenty of time to make any reasonable modifications they were going to require in order to proceed with the project.

After an uneventful flight from Minneapolis and no delayed baggage, I checked into the Saint Marie, grabbed a quick sandwich from room service, and called home. The bright red numbers on the face of the clock radio on the nightstand indicated it was 10:55 p.m. I hadn't been able to connect with Yawdy since we'd eaten gumbo and had one too many beers at his place a couple of months earlier. The old guy didn't have an answering machine, so there was no way to leave a message. I didn't have his niece's phone number as an alternative.

Eleven o'clock was early for New Orleans, so I figured a quick trip to Preservation Hall was in order. A light warm rain began to splatter my glasses as I walked down river along Bourbon Street from the Saint Marie. I turned right on Saint Peter and stopped outside the rusty iron gate of the Hall. I was surprised to see Adrian sitting in the old captain's chair in the carriage way. She seemed equally startled with my presence.

"Well, hi. We haven't seen you for a while," she said.

"I haven't been around for a couple of months. What are you doing working over here tonight? I recall a little stocky fellow with a T-shirt a couple of sizes too small working the entryway to the Hall."

"Oh, that's Johnny. He's taking it easy tonight. He's got problems with his ol' knees. I'm his fill-in."

"That's quite a hat you've got on tonight," I remarked.

A striking scarlet red straw pork pie hat sat tilted low on Adrian's brow. She had to peek out from under the brim to see. The iridescent eye of a peacock feather protruded from the faded hat band.

"It's Johnny's pork pie, but he lets me wear it. He says I bring him luck. I think the ol' coot just likes the smell of my perfume."

"It looks great on you, Adrian. I think you ought to wear it all the time."

"Oh, yeah, right."

She arose from the old captain's chair with its faded chipped, and cracked white paint and stepped to the center of the carriage way. As she did, the chair rolled back against the wall from the slope of the floor.

"How late are they going to play?" I asked.

"Usually about 12:30, but it's been slow tonight, so they might end a little earlier."

"Bourbon Street was quiet tonight walking over here," I said.

"With as much rain as we've had the last few days you'd think it's already hurricane season."

"I read a long range forecast the other day that said it's going to be a busy year for hurricanes. Have you ever been here when one hit?"

"No, sir, I'm a big chicken. I always go up to Jackson to stay with my brother. It gives me a good excuse to get out of here for a few days."

"Where's your Uncle Yawdy hiding out? I haven't been able to catch him at home, and lord knows he doesn't have an answering machine."

"He's in Memphis. An old friend of his passed away this week. He went up to the funeral."

"I'm sorry."

"Oh, that's okay. Uncle Yawdy's got lots of old friends dying off. He said he stopped reading the obits in the newspaper 'cause he was afraid he'd see his own name."

"How's he been feeling?"

"Good, as long as I can keep him taking his medication. That's a chore."

"Are you a musician, Adrian?"

"Me? Hardly, Uncle Yawdy says I'd break both my legs if I tried to carry a tune."

I chuckled. She was a friendly person, bore a strong resemblance to her uncle, and had the same broad smile and glitter in her eyes as Yawdy. Her long, slender arms stuck out from the short sleeve gray Preservation Hall T-shirt she was wearing. She may have not been able to carry a tune, but she was certainly a natural beauty. The earthy scent of her perfume carried on the breeze filtering through the carriage way.

"The T-shirt must be the required dress for working out here, huh?"

"Oh, this," she looked down as she grabbed the T-shirt and bloused it out from her body.

"I'd like to buy a ticket from you to sit in and listen for a little while."

"It's on me tonight. Make yourself at home, Mike."

I stepped into the doorway of the Hall. The mild fragrance of wood, sweat, and aging sheetrock lingered in the air. A middle-aged couple, sitting on one of the wooden benches near the doorway gave a hand gesture indicating they could slide over a bit, if I wanted to squeeze in next to them. I spotted a place to sit in front of them on the floor if I didn't mind sharing the faded cushion with Champ, the resident feline. I nodded my head to the couple on the bench and pointed to the cushion. I picked up the old cat and sat him on my lap. Cosmo recognized me and gave a quick wink. The slide on his trombone reached nearly where I was sitting. I didn't recognize the song they were playing.

It seemed strange to see someone else in Yawdy's chair on the clarinet. I hadn't been to the Hall that many times, but had grown accustomed to seeing Yawdy's smiling, weaving, bobbing enthusiasm driving the band. His replacement was a much more laid-back performer. He played with his eyes closed, inwardly focused on the music. He looked to be thirty years Yawdy's junior. The cool notes rolled out of his shiny clarinet and seemed to hang on Cosmo's brassy trombone.

Zeb's bright blue and orange necktie danced from side to side as he bobbed and weaved from one song to the next on his trumpet. His white dress shirt glistened from the sweat soaking through. He announced each of the songs in Yawdy's absence. When they played "Back Porch," he told a story about his grandmother and the forty or so cats she fed on the back porch with goat milk. Zeb said his job was to milk the old goat. He said everything went fine until one day he tied up the ol' Billy. Cats clamoring close by ended up getting kicked over the back fence. Zeb said that was the end of his goat milking. Stories and songs, they flowed together like the fine weave on a carpet. As Yawdy said, "New Orleans jazz was all about life." That was clearly the case this night.

I was startled a bit as Zeb came off his chair, stood up with his trumpet, thanked everyone for coming, and announced the time had come to head the horses to the barn. He began a count to kick off the last number.

"One, two, three, four…" And started singing. "*Oh, when the saints, go marchin' in, oh, when the saints go marchin' in, oh, Lord, I wanna be in that number, When the saints go marchin' in…*"

He put the horn back up to his lips and gave the song an extra kick as he started a slow shuffling step-by-step march out of the Hall. Gigi laid his bass against the wall and began clapping as he followed Zeb to the doorway. One by one, they filed out of the Hall until Ada was the only one left at the piano. She led one final chorus as she slid her chair back and stood up while she continued playing. The small crowd in the room burst with applause, acknowledging the gifts the band shared—gifts of music and love. Ada turned, gave a slight bow and then joined her fellow musicians in the carriage way. The procession then retired to the recesses of Preservation Hall.

When the room cleared, I stood up still holding onto Champ and surveyed my surroundings. I thought about the foresight of the founders of the Hall, the gift they had given both the public and the musicians by providing such a wonderful place. What an amazing setting for the preservation of an important piece of African-American history.

I walked out of the doorway to the Hall as Adrian looked my way.

"You'll be covered with cat hair."

"Oh, that's okay. I guess I'm a pushover when it comes to an old tomcat."

The old white cat gave a raspy meow as I set him down in the carriage way. In a flash he bolted through the open wrought iron gate and out onto the sidewalk.

"He's got lots of lady friends in the Quarter," Adrian offered as she put her hands on her hips and looked a bit perturbed that Champ took off so quickly. "I thought you two might be staying in there all night."

"Nah, just soaking in the place," I said. "The band kind of skedaddled out of here this evening."

"Oh, they like to do that on the Saints."

"Do you have to close up the place?"

"No, not tonight. Emmett and Cosmo will lock up."

"Are you up for a coffee and an order over at Du Monde's? If you've got time, I'll buy."

"Sure, I'd do that. Just a minute and I'll grab my bag."

Adrian locked the cabinet where she had been sitting, picked up an oversized braided blue and red handbag, and hung the pork pie hat on a hook next to the doorway into the Hall. She spun around and looked my way, "I'm ready if you are."

We walked towards front o' town on Saint Peter and along the side of Jackson Square.

"I've enjoyed getting to know your uncle," I said.

"Yes, I'm lucky to have him. I know he enjoys you, too."

"We've had some good visits."

"Didn't you two meet on a plane or something?"

For the next few minutes I gave Adrian a recount of my and Yawdy's first meeting, the connection with my relatives, and how much I valued his friendship.

We walked across Decatur and turned left towards Café Du Monde. I inhaled deeply to take in the aroma of fresh hot cooked dough. "How does a person ever walk by this place, and not go in for a fresh, hot order?"

"Can't be done," she added.

We took an open table just inside the doorway. Adrian hooked her handbag over the corner of her chair and sat with her back to the pay phones just inside the arched French doors. She untied the green and black bandana holding her hair in a ponytail and gave her head a quick shake. She had a full head of wavy, coal black hair.

In no time at all we had two steaming cups of chicory coffee and an order of snow-covered beignets patiently waiting on the table in front of us. I slid the plate across the table and offered Adrian first choice.

"Uncle Yawdy calls these French fritters."

"How's that?" I asked.

"Beignet is the French word for fritter."

"Do you know how they became such a special New Orleans icon?"

"French colonists brought the custom of serving special sweet treats with them to the new country, and I'm glad they did."

"Me, too."

Soon we were both licking sticky powdered sugar off our fingers. How the sugar gets everywhere when the beignet melts the moment it hits your tongue was beyond both of us.

"I missed Yawdy's presence tonight," I commented, "He's some kind of musician."

"I assume he has told you about his life?"

"Yes, bits and pieces."

"My Uncle Yawdy is an amazing man. I know he could have been famous if he wanted to."

"He showed me some pictures over at the jazz archives on the campus of Tulane the last time I was in town. It looked like he's played with some pretty famous musicians."

"Oh, yes," she added.

"Even Louis Armstrong."

"My dad said Satchmo loved my uncle. He begged Uncle Yawdy to stay with him. Said he'd basically give him the moon if he would."

"But he felt the need to be here in New Orleans?"

"Yes, he did. I guess my uncle was never really taken up with the lure of fame and fortune."

"He told me he decided to come back to New Orleans and make his life here because of what he saw happen to other musicians on the road."

"Yes, I think that's true."

"He's referred to some type of secret."

"A secret? In what regard?"

"I'm not certain. I can't get him to tell me."

"What do you think it could be?"

"I think his secret is that a person needs to have the courage to make a change, to pursue what they feel passionate about in life. But that's really no secret."

As I looked into Adrian's deep brown eyes, I felt like I was talking to Yawdy.

"Do you know if that's it, Adrian?"

"I think you will have to ask my Uncle Yawdy."

"No luck so far; I've tried. I get a sort of run around."

"Well, Mike, maybe he's trying to pick the right time to share it with you."

"How's that, Adrian?"

"Uncle Yawdy considers his secret one of the most valuable things in the world. I think he's discovered something in life most of us miss."

"He told me we've all heard it and not once but literally a thousand times, yet we've missed it," I remarked.

"My Uncle Yawdy has a storehouse of wisdom locked up in that noggin of his."

"Adrian, you seem to be as elusive as your uncle."

"Mike, my uncle likes you."

"It's mutual."

"Maybe he's trying to sense the right time to share his secret with you."

"Maybe not. He's no spring chicken."

"I think he'll be around for a while," she added.

"You gonna eat that last beignet?"

"Nope, that one's got your name on it."

"When will your uncle get back in town?"

"I think sometime this weekend. Are you going to be around?"

"No. I'll be home in Minnesota this weekend. I won't be back to New Orleans till late August."

"You should call my uncle and make arrangements to get together. If you can't catch him you can try my number, and I can relay the message. She swung her handbag around from the side of the chair and retrieved a pencil and some paper from inside. When she'd finished writing down the number she handed the paper to me.

"Thank you, Adrian. I'll do that."

"No problem. Glad to help."

"Adrian."

"Yes."

"I can't tell you how much I respect your Uncle Yawdy."

"I know; I do, too. We all do."

NINETEEN

Checking In

"Jazz is the only art form existing today in which there is freedom of individual without the loss of group contact."

—Dave Brubeck

The light gray overstuffed chair enveloped me as I sat staring into the pearly New York City lights beyond the rain-splattered window. The Waldorf Astoria wasn't a place I normally stayed in Manhattan, but because I had a meeting the next morning a few blocks away, it made the most sense. Our attorneys had filed an action with the advertising council of the Better Business Bureau against a competitor for claims they were making in the marketplace; hopefully the meeting tomorrow would be the end of the matter. I expected a steamy August walk over to Thirty-Sixth Street in Midtown. I had a headache that was throbbing like a diesel pile driver, banging away on a steel bridge piling. On the phone, it sounded like my wife was dealing with a pile driver of her own.

"I had the meeting today with Patrick's team about the summer school."

"How did it go?"

"I wish you could just sit in on one and meet the team of people it takes to manage a special needs child. There were eleven people in the room with me. All of them providing so much information, it made my head spin.

"I think you need a pay increase."

"Oh yeah, like the pay in this job is any good at all."

"You do a great job with it, Sharon."

"How did the plant tours go this time?" she asked.

"I like Yawdy's term."

"What's that?"

"Humbug. I think when you are on the outs with your boss, every damn thing you say or do can get you in trouble. Being tired on top of it doesn't help."

"These trips always take it out of you."

"I can't imagine why! We've only been in eight states and to both coasts in the last five days. We've been up and going by 5:00 a.m. every morning, and there has been the usual pontification dinner every night. Sharon, the people above me never tire of listening to themselves talk—from the time we hop on board the corporate jet in the morning to the wee hours of the night, all that's talked about is business."

"Wasn't New York your first stop on Monday?"

"Yes. We were up at the plant in the Finger Lakes region near Ithaca. Then over the course of the week we've stopped in salt facilities across the country all the way to California."

"What was the weather like in San Francisco?"

"Rain. It's rained on us everywhere we've been this week."

"Do you even know what time zone you are in?"

"Hardly."

"Why did you go back to New York?" she asked.

"It's the final meeting tomorrow with the national advertising review board. I caught a commercial flight out of San Jose to make it back here."

"Oh, yeah, you told me that."

"If everything goes as planned, I should get back to the Twin Cities tomorrow night, but I don't get in until after 11:00 p.m."

"That's late."

"I'll tell you, dear, I'm ready to bail out of this level of a commitment to the corporation."

"Oh, yeah, I'd like to resign from this single-parent gig myself."

"I'm serious, I'm completely frustrated. My boss and I are at odds on nearly every issue that comes up. He says up, and I say down; he says black, and I say white. He might know the trading businesses he came from, but he doesn't have a clue about what it takes to run a sales organization, let alone a salt company. The guy above him is even worse. I've never seen individuals so full of themselves."

"Are you still going to Louisiana next week?"

"Yes, why?"

"It's just that there have been so many hurricanes this summer. I was wondering if you could wait until a little later in the season."

"Hopefully, I can get in and out between storms."

"I have to go, Hun. I've got a couple of calls to make, then I need to get Patrick headed for bed. Then I've got to drag myself out of bed in the morning and go through another day on this end with that boy. God knows I love him, but damn, he's a challenge."

The phone clicked as she hung up. The call at the end of the day always made the distance seem further. Even after thirty years, it never got any easier. I went back to the love fest with my e-mail when my cell phone rang.

"Yawdy Rum, what are you up to this evening?"

"Just checkin' on you. Makin' sure you ain't gettin' in no trouble out there."

"Me? Ah, come on, Yawdy."

"Where abouts you at tonight, Mister Mike?"

"I'm in Manhattan."

"Where you stayin'?"

"The Waldorf."

"Well, now, ain't you a fat cat."

"Yeah, I'm glad I'm not paying for it."

"That's a fine hotel. How long you stayin' there?" he asked.

"I'm only here one night. I've been on a whirlwind trip all across the country this week. I had to come back into Manhattan for a meeting I've got in the morning."

"Is your dog gonna know you when you get home?"

"If I'm lucky," I answered.

"Do you know what it means to take a little time to rest? With all your comin's and goin's I don't see how you keep get time to catch your breath. You know, Mister Mike, even when I'm playin' in the band, and I'm often sittin' down, I gotta take a rest, all the band members do. Ain't no one can go a hundred miles an hour all the time."

"Yawdy, I don't think I do a very good job in that area."

"Are you carryin' any sheet music with you on the road this week?"

"Yes. I've got some in my briefcase," I answered.

"Well, you take it out and give it a good look. You need to pay attention as to how many rests are in that piece of music. Takin' time to rest adds dimension to the music and gives you time to catch your breath. The same is true for life."

He paused a moment on the phone to drive home his point and then he continued. "I got your note in the mail. Sorry I missed you last time you were down here. Adrian said you came by the Hall one night. Are you still comin' this way next weekend?" he asked.

"Yes. I'm flying into Lafayette on the corporate jet for a meeting on Friday morning. I'll pick up a rental car and drive over to New Orleans Friday night."

"How long are you gonna be here?"

"I'm headed home early Sunday morning. I have a presentation to deliver Saturday to a trade group at the Marriott. I'm hoping to get in and out between the storms you all keep having down there."

"Oh, boy, we've sure had a rash of 'em this summer. Gonna have any free time?"

"A little bit. I was hoping we could hook up for an early dinner Saturday?"

"Elizabeth's?" he asked.

"Tell them to get the pu pu platter ready. I'll pick you up at your place. How about five-thirty?"

TWENTY

Dissonance

"It's taken all my life to learn what not to play."

—Dizzy Gillespie

I arrived at the corporate hangar at the Twin Cities airport before any of the other passengers. I found the flight roster on a clipboard hanging next to the doorway of the coffee room. Two additional names had been added in pencil to the typed roster of the entourage going to Louisiana. I recognized one of the names as the senior corporate HR manager. There could only be one reason she was joining us for the trip. I figured before the day was over, I'd know why.

The glistening oval windows on the company's private jet provided a wide angle view of the lazy Mississippi River some forty thousand feet below us as we flew south. Faint wisps of pure white clouds scattered across an endless deep blue horizon. I nibbled on the grapes and finished most of the yogurt, but left the rest of the breakfast untouched the flight crew had for us on the jet when we boarded in Minneapolis. The coffee, usually quite tasty, was bitter. I leaned back into the comfort of the oversized soft leather captain's chair in the rear of the passenger cabin and attempted to put the pieces of the day together in my mind.

Conflicting travel schedules made it impossible to get my performance review scheduled with my boss. We finally agreed to conduct it while we were together in Louisiana. Lately, we'd been like two fighting cocks circling each other in the ring, neither really wanting to engage, yet unable to avoid what was about to happen.

Except for a few bumps on approach and a short delay in taxing once we were on the ground, the landing at the Lafayette Regional Airport was routine. We boarded a pre-arranged van, and in less than twenty minutes arrived at the plant. The plant tour proved uneventful and the facility review meeting ended by mid-afternoon. Now, here we were, four of us sitting face-to-face in a stuffy, dark walnut paneled plant conference room on the second floor of the plant offices. I sat in a stiff, upright chair facing a round glass-topped conference table, my stone-faced boss positioned on my left, one of his henchmen sat across from me, and the HR manager to my right. They had their backs to a glary sun-drenched floor-to-ceiling window. I had to squint a bit to really see their faces.

My boss spouted off, "You are not supporting our new structure. You have not followed my directions. You have no integrity."

This sure didn't start out as the usual performance review. I could feel the sweat running down inside my cotton shirt. Integrity, hell, this guy couldn't spell the word. I felt hot all over. I was mad enough to reach across the table and punch his lights out. I could feel my heart racing in my chest. He didn't have a clue. Here sat someone across from me who didn't have the slightest idea of how to build a team. Here was someone so paranoid, so insecure, he was paralyzed. I slowly counted in my mind—*one—two—three—relax, Mike,* I said to myself, *You've handled more difficult situations than this.*

I began slowly. "This is not about results; it's about style. You don't like the way I get things done. You're intimidated by my depth of knowledge and experience in the salt industry. I even think you resent the respect I've earned from the people is this organization. You confuse my passion for this business with arrogance. We simply see things differently. However, I can tell this is not about an appraisal this afternoon."

"No, it's not," he snapped.

His voice quivered. The other two sat with their backs erect in jaw-clenching silence. The senior HR manager, a plump middle-aged woman with squinty little eyes, and bottle-brown frizzy hair, and a short skirt nervously fidgeted with a lead pencil. The other gentleman across the table from me pursed his lips, squeezing the blood out into his cheeks, doing everything he could in order to not make eye contact with me. The air felt thick, heavy, and seemed to retard every word spoken. My boss handed me a document that outlined the separation terms the corporation was offering. He started through the document in a rushed manner, only mentioning key words and phrases.

I stopped him, "Excuse me. Are you expecting me to sign this today?" I asked.

"No. We're going to place you on a thirty-day leave to evaluate our offer. We understand, however, you have a speaking engagement in New Orleans this weekend on behalf of the company. We are aware of your position in the trade association and understand the engagement cannot be changed. We'll start the clock on Monday."

I picked my briefcase up off the floor where it was sitting next to my chair. I slid my materials off the table and dropped them into the bulging black case. I could see the glistening beads of moisture on the glass table top, where my boss had his hand lying only a few seconds earlier. His face was beet red and his lips were tight. I stood up, reached across the table, shook hands with each of them, and said, "I'll be in touch." I turned, left the room, and headed for a spare office in the building. I'd used it earlier in the day to make a couple of calls. The dried leather creaked as I let my weight settle back into the desk chair. I took a deep, long breath. So, this was it, thirty-three years in the industry, and I end it being flown in a twenty-five million dollar jet to the gallows. But I was surprised at how I felt. Not sad, not disappointed, more like a burden had been lifted from my shoulders. Nothing I had seen from those at the very top of the organization appealed to me. The political nonsense and insecure personalities were nauseating. This offered a chance to move on and do something else with the rest of my life.

My administrative assistant still carrying a bright yellow hard hat and wearing safety glasses from the plant tour she'd been on, stepped into the door of the office.

"Mike, I wanted to catch you before I left."

"No problem, Suzy, what can I do for you?"

"Well, first, thanks for asking me to come along. I got to see the whole operation today."

"How did it go?" I asked.

"Fantastic. I never realized how complex it is to make something as simple as salt. It's just something people take for granted."

"I'm glad you enjoyed it."

"Mike, you're headed from here on to New Orleans, correct?"

"Right."

"Do you need anything else from me for the presentation?"

"Nope, I'm all set. Thanks."

She glanced around the room. "Didn't this used to be your office at one time?"

"Yes, it was. I was a field sales manager for many years. In hindsight, I'd probably be better off had I stayed in the field. The distance served me well."

"You had your evaluation this afternoon, didn't you?"

"Yes."

"How did it…," she stopped in mid-sentence. "Don't tell me, we can talk next week."

"Enjoy your trip back on the jet, Suzy. It's a first-class way to travel."

"Good luck in New Orleans, Mike, and keep a close eye on the weather. They are forecasting some nasty stuff."

"How's that?"

"When we were on the plant tour we stopped in the main plant ops room and watched something on television from the National Hurricane Center on a storm off the coast of Florida. They are saying it may come this way."

"My flight is out early Sunday morning. I'll be fine. I've been coming down here on and off for almost thirty years and haven't gotten caught by a hurricane yet."

"Well, I'll see you next week."

She turned and left the office. At that point I was simply thinking about Sharon. I'd told her I suspected something was in the wind to get me to leave. But I needed to get through the presentation in

New Orleans and connect with Yawdy before flying home on Sunday. I heard someone at the door and glanced up to see Grantland. He was holding the keys to the rental car he picked up for me to drive to New Orleans.

"Here are the car keys, Mike. There's a brand new white Impala waiting for you in the visitor's slot in the front lot. It's all set up for you to drop it off at National in New Orleans. The paperwork is above the visor."

"Thanks, Grantland, I appreciate your help on the car and making sure this office was available for me today."

"It's yours as long as you need it. After a day like this with all you corporate seagulls here, this ol' Cajun is heading home."

"I know; we fly in, eat your food, squawk like hell, and crap all over the place. Right?"

"Pretty much sums it up."

He started to leave, and then spun back into the office holding onto the doorjamb as he leaned back in.

"One more thing, Mike, you might keep a close watch out on the weather, and if you can leave New Orleans early, I think I'd do it."

"Suzy mentioned something about a storm off the Florida coast," I said.

"It's looking like it could be here in our backyard on Monday."

"I'm out early Sunday morning. I should be okay."

"Are you hooking up with your jazz buddy in the Quarter?"

"I wouldn't miss the chance."

I closed the door as soon as he had gone then sat back down in the warm leather chair. I spent the next several minutes slowly reading through the agreement I'd been given. I disconnected my computer from the network, wrapped up the power cable, and put the remaining items in my briefcase. The outer office was empty when I stepped into the lobby and walked out the front door to the parking lot. I was looking forward to the drive to New Orleans. I needed time to think.

The traffic on I-10 was heavier than usual, specifically trucks, one after another. I imagined the storm damage from Hurricane Dennis that had hit Florida a month or so earlier created a windfall for companies who could move materials into the affected areas.

I flipped open my cell and placed a call home.

"How is it going on your end?" I asked, never really knowing if I was ready for Sharon's response.

"Where are you?"

"I'm about twenty miles east of Baton Rouge on I-10 with what seems like a million trucks going the same way."

"I'm sorry, you cut out on me a bit," she responded.

"I said, 'I'm on I-10 about twenty miles east of Baton Rouge'."

"Are you staying in New Orleans tonight?"

"Yes."

"Maybe it would be better if we talked when you get to your room."

"Why's that?"

"Patrick wrote a note and took it to summer school today."

"That doesn't sound so bad. What's up?"

"The note said he wanted to kill himself. He gave it to another student."

I felt the rumble strips on the side of the highway send a vibration through the car as I pulled over to the side of the interstate and brought the Impala to a stop on the shoulder. I wanted to focus on the call. My stomach had that warm queasy feeling you get right before you feel like you are going to throw up.

"Did the school call you to let you know?"

"Yes. This is going to get really involved."

"This isn't the first time for a note like this, but it's been a while, huh," I offered hesitantly.

"I'm frustrated. I know we try to help him in so many ways, but when it comes to this, I'm at a loss to know how to help. I don't think Patrick really means it, but I don't know for sure. It scares me."

"Did you talk to him?"

"Not yet. His life skills coach picked him up at school for the usual session they have scheduled. I'm expecting him home any time now. Where are …"

The phone cut out.

"I'm sorry, Sharon, I didn't catch what you asked. The phone cut out on you."

"Where are you staying?" she repeated.

"I'm at the Saint Marie."

"How did it go…"

The phone kept crackling.

"What was that?"

"How did it go today?"

"Not very good on my end either."

"What …"

She cut out again.

"Not very good," I repeated.

I held on the phone for a few seconds, not knowing for sure if I still had a connection or not, when Sharon came back on the phone.

"It was Patrick on the other line. Something has changed, and I've got to run and pick him up. Call you later."

Maybe it was better we were interrupted. She had enough to manage on her end. There would be lots of time to talk later.

It was after 9:30 p.m. when I pulled the rental car up in front of the hotel. I opened the door just as the bellman stepped around from behind the car. My glasses immediately fogged over from the wave of humidity riding on intense Gulf heat that hit me as I got out of the Impala. I raised my glasses, and placed them on top of my head so I could see."

"Good evenin'. And w'lcome to da Saint Marie. May I hep you wit yo bags, sir?"

"Sure, let me pop the trunk."

I reached back in the car and pushed the trunk unlock button on the key ring I'd left on the dashboard. I grabbed my sport coat and stepped around the back of the car and on to the sidewalk.

"Don't you be da fellow dat always be havin' dat guitar ova yo shoulder?"

"Good memory. This is kind of a whirlwind trip this time. I had to leave it at home."

"Where you be comin' from dis evenin'?"

"I drove over from Lafayette."

"You been listenin' to dat radio?"

"Uh, no, actually I haven't."

"Den you might want ta check wit de desk clerk 'cause dem autorities been talkin' 'bout a bad hurricane may come dis way. You may want ta hightail it out'a here a bit early."

"I'm out on Sunday morning."

"Ah, den you be okay."

TWENTY-ONE

No Way Out!

"An 'all dat Big Box axes
When time comes fo' to go,
Lemme be wid old Jazzbo"

—Sterling Brown

There was no use losing my temper with the frazzled agent. Undoubtedly, other exasperated travelers had clawed the deep wrinkles in her face. I adjusted my watchband and glanced at the time. It was just past 10:00 p.m. on Sunday evening. I had been at the airport for nearly eighteen hours trying to get out of New Orleans.

"I'm sorry, but right now it doesn't look like there are any seats available."

"Do you have any idea what happened to my reservation?"

"I can't tell, sir. I've entered the ticket number you gave me again, but we don't have any record of your reservation in our system."

I looked back at the agent who seemed to be aging in front of me. "Well, my original ticket this morning was one-way. I almost never do that. I imagine that's what screwed it up. Any idea how far you are overbooked on the next flight and whether going stand-by is even an option?"

"No, sir, I'm sorry. It seems to be changing by the minute, and it's getting so late, we are running out of options."

"What are your operations people saying?" I asked.

"We are hearing the authorities are going to close the airport."

"Close the airport! How the hell can they do that? This place is packed."

"Sir, I believe they will be passing out cots and blankets."

"Can you help me with anything out of Baton Rouge, Lafayette, or maybe even Houston?"

The gate agent with her thin puckered lips, replied, "Baton Rouge and Lafayette are both in the same situation as we are here. If you could drive to Houston, you might be able to get something."

"I heard that I-10 is a parking lot," I added.

"I'm sure that's the case, sir."

I stepped away from the ticket counter at the Northwest gate and looked up at a television suspended from the ceiling in the waiting area. There was a swelling group of travelers underneath it huddled in a cloud of fear. A rather perturbed-looking redheaded lady standing near the back of the group swung around and looked my way. I quizzed her as to what she had just heard the announcer on CNN report.

"They said the hurricane has been upgraded to a category five storm," she said, "and it looks like it's going to hit here in the morning. Someone just got this from a Delta captain who was standing here with us a few minutes ago." She handed me a thin, crinkled sheet of auto-feed printer paper and then stammered a bit as she said, "I don't know if you want to read it or not."

I took the delicate paper in my hands and began reading.

URGENT–WEATHER MESSAGE–NAT'L WEATHER SERVICE. NEW ORLEANS. 08:45 PM CDT SUN AUG 28 2005
...DEVASTATING DAMAGE EXPECTED...
HURRICANE KATRINA...A MOST POWERFUL HURRICANE WITH UNPRECEDENTED STRENGTH...RIVALING THE INTENSITY OF HURRICANE CAMILLE OF 1969...TO MAKE LANDFALL ALONG NEW ORLEANS DELTA DAYLIGHT HOURS MON AUG 29.
MOST OF THE AREA WILL BE UNINHABITABLE FOR WEEKS...PERHAPS LONGER...

It outlined that over half of even well-constructed homes were likely to be destroyed, most industrial buildings would be damaged, and the danger from flying debris would place persons, pets, and livestock in peril. Power outages were likely to persist for weeks and potable water would be unavailable.

"Well, isn't this special. If they knew this was such a potentially dangerous storm, why the hell did they wait so long to put out a message like this?"

"You're telling me. Where are you trying to go?" she asked.

"Minneapolis, but I haven't had any luck all day. How about you?"

"Montreal," she said, as she waved her ticket jacket in my face. "This is the third flight we've tried. We've gotten bumped off the others. They are all overbooked. We are hoping this one works. They say it's probably the last flight that will get out."

"I've been here for over eighteen hours. The place was a zoo even at 4:30 a.m. this morning. Have you been here all day?"

"Same for us," she remarked, as she pointed down to a tired looking eight- or nine-year-old girl with the same color of red hair and a face full of freckles sitting on the floor next to her. "My niece and I've been here all day."

I was startled by the ring on my cell phone. Since late afternoon all I'd been able to get was an "all circuits are busy" message anytime I tried to place a call.

"Hello."

"Hello, Mister Mike."

"Why, Yawdy Rum. I wondered what happened to you. It's good to hear your voice. Man, has it ever been nuts here. I called several times yesterday but could never catch you. When you didn't answer your phone today, I figured you left town with Adrian."

"Where 'bouts you at, Mister Mike?"

"I'm still at the airport in New Orleans, and it doesn't look like I'm going anywhere. How about you, are you in Jackson?"

"Nope, I'm sittin' here in my kitchen restin' my bones just a bit."

It felt like the bottom dropped out of my stomach, "In your kitchen, what the hell, man, are you crazy? They've upgraded the storm to a category five hurricane, and they think New Orleans is going to take a direct hit."

"Guess that means both of us better hunker down a bit."

"Yawdy, I'll tell you what. It doesn't look like I'm going to be flying out. All the flights today have been overbooked, and now they say they are going to close the airport. Let me see if anyone has any rental cars left. If I can get a one, I'll come and get you, and we'll head down to Avery Island. There is an emergency shelter above ground at the mine. We ought to be able to make it over there in a couple of hours, three at the most. If I can't get a car, then you're right, we better all learn how to hunker down."

He didn't answer, "Yawdy, are you there?"

"Yep, I'm here, Mister Mike. Just thinkin'."

"How about you do your thinking with me while we are in the car?"

"Okay, I'll be here. Come on by."

"Yawdy, you might want to throw a change of clothes or two in a suitcase to take with you."

I grabbed my briefcase, threw it on top of my roller bag, and headed back to the main terminal. I opened my cell phone and hit the speed dial for National's emerald customer emergency travel line. It took four attempts but the call finally went through. I gave the operator my priority account number and held as I listened to the agent tapping out my request on her keyboard. The delay seemed like an eternity.

"Looks like you are in luck. They should have a full sized sedan for you at the Emerald Aisle, Mr. Lane, but I'd suggest you get right over there 'cause it sounds as if it's nuts down there. You don't want that car to get away. Are you ready for the reservation number?"

"Hang on just a minute and I'll get some paper."

I called home on a pay phone in the rental car office while I was waiting to get the car. I assured Sharon the shelter at the mine would be a safe place to ride out the storm, although, I don't think she believed me. I knew she would be dealing with a challenge from Patrick because my schedule had changed, not to mention the note he'd written. Sharon and I had talked a few times during the day when I could get my phone to work. Mostly we talked about the company's offer and what it meant for both of us if I accepted it. She wasn't surprised they wanted me out. She knew how much passion I had for the business and how I had constantly challenged the direction they were taking the company. She said I had outgrown the place. We talked about Patrick, about the note he had written. While she was concerned, she said she didn't believe he really meant it. It was just his autistic way of communicating his feelings of frustration and lack of being understood by others. In his own way, it got him attention.

It had taken over two hours, but finally, I was behind the wheel of what looked like the very same non-descript white Chevy Impala I had turned in some twenty hours ago. Or, was it the day before? I'd been at the airport so damn long trying to get out before the hurricane, the day had blurred. It had been raining on and off lightly for several hours, but now the rain seemed to be picking up in intensity. The green LED light on the face of the radio said it was 12:55 a.m. It was Monday morning, and I'd hoped to be back in Minnesota.

Two lanes of red taillights stretched ahead of me on I-10 as far as I could see as I drove towards the city. Things had just turned bonkers in New Orleans. It was like a city under siege, like an exodus in the face of an advancing army. By the time I made it to the I-610 split, I hoped to turn into the city, but the police had all lanes blocked and were routing traffic east. I inched along I-10 all the way out to Crowder. An exasperated looking Louisiana state trooper, who was attempting to block the exit ramp at Crowder, was in some type of argument with a fellow in an old beat-up green Dodge pickup with Guadalajara license plates and a back end full of stepladders. I couldn't leave Yawdy. I took a chance, spun the Impala around from the center lane, and shot down the ramp. I figured if I could make it off the interstate, I might be able to sneak my way back into the Quarter.

It was nearly three in the morning when I turned off of Elysian Fields onto Chartres. I flipped open my cell phone, prayed for a signal, and dialed Yawdy's number again. I'd been trying to call him ever since I left the airport but kept getting an equipment busy signal. I got a ring.

"Come on, Mr. Rum, answer the phone, buddy," I said to myself as the ring crackled in the earpiece.

"Hello."

"Hello, Yawdy, it's Mike."

"What time is it?"

I gave the clock on the face of the radio a quick glance. "It's about 2:00 a.m."

"After your last call, I got everythin' together I need. I've never been to a salt mine, but if you still think that's the best thin' to do, I guess I'm up for it."

"Did you hear anything from anyone else at the Hall?"

"No. I'm thinkin' they all left town."

"Yawdy, I'm having a hard time hearing you. I should be out front in just a few minutes. Don't come out. I'll come to the house and get you."

"Okay, I got the light on."

It was raining harder than I had ever seen and the wind was whipping the car so much it was all I could do to keep it in the middle of the street. I pulled up in front of what I thought was Yawdy's house and parked against the curb going the wrong way. At least I was headed into the wind when I opened the door. A drenching wave came off the windshield with each pass of the wipers. I made a mad dash for Yawdy's porch, but got knocked down by the wind before I made it to the railing. I pulled myself up along the edge of the steps and jumped up on the porch. Yawdy, standing in the doorway, pushed open the screen door as I lunged inside.

"Man, is it blowin' screamers out there or what?" he hollered.

"Hey, old man, it's good to see you."

"I didn't think you were goin' to make it, Mister Mike."

"I was beginning to have doubts myself. It's bad and getting worse out there. We got to get going, Yawdy."

He bent over, grabbed his suitcase, his horn case, and pulled his beret down tight on his head.

"Here, let me carry that suitcase. You hold onto your clarinet case, my arm, and don't let go. You got it."

"Lead the way, man."

Yawdy hit the light switch in the living room just as something outside on the street exploded with a brilliant flash. It looked as if a power pole with a transformer had fallen along the other side of the Chartres. Bright white electricity danced along the sidewalk on the opposite side of the street. We could hear the snapping and popping of the electricity over the howling wind. The electricity went off, and the whole area became a dark swirling mass of wind and rain. We stepped out on the porch with Yawdy hanging on to my left arm. One thing was certain, the old guy had a grip. We made it to the car, I pulled open the passenger door, and leaned into it with my shoulder to hold it open. I screamed, "GET IN, YAWDY." He let go of my arm and slid behind me into the seat. I opened the rear door and threw his suitcase into the backseat.

We pulled away from the curb but hadn't quite made it to the end of the block when Yawdy grabbed me by the arm, and said, "Mister Mike, we gotta go back, I forgot somethin'."

"Yawdy, it's too late now."

"No, Mister Mike, please, we gotta go back. There is another case sittin' just inside the door. It's a small black horn case, an old one. You gotta get that case for me."

"Yawdy, you got your horn case right there on the floorboard. We didn't forget it."

"No, there is another one. It's right inside the door. We gotta get it. The door is unlocked."

I looked at the determination in his eyes, put the car in reverse, and we backed down the street. When we were back in front of his house, I slammed the car into park, opened the door, and made the dash up to Yawdy's porch. It was all I could do to see the steps. The rain felt like a million bumblebees, all stinging at the same time. The wind whistled through the screen door as I pushed it open against the wind. The doorknob was wet and slippery as I rotated it, pushed the door open, and stepped into the living room.

The room was pitch black. I dropped to my hands and knees and began feeling all around the small entryway. I'd crawled five or six feet along the floor, nearly to the couch, with my hands sweeping back and forth in front of me, trying to find the case. When my hand finally made contact with it, I knocked it across the hardwood floor, and under the coffee table. I extended my fingers in the darkness searching along the braided rug under the table. I felt it. I didn't know what kind of horn could be this important, but then again, I wasn't an old jazz musician.

I pulled Yawdy's front door shut just as the wind tore the outer screen door off the hinges, and sailed it off the end of the porch. Leaning into the wind, I struggled back to the Impala. I opened the door on the car, collapsed into the seat, and handed the tattered black horn case to Yawdy. He wrapped his arms around the case and held it close to his chest.

"Yawdy, I don't think we can make it out of town to the housing at the mine. It's just too dangerous. Have you got any suggestions?"

"How about the Hall?"

"Do you have a key?"

"Yep."

He reached into his pants pocket and handed me a rusty old skeleton key.

"It fits the front gate into the carriage way. I brought it just in case," he said.

"Well, if we can get it open, maybe we're in business."

I put the car in drive and tried to wipe the water off my face with my handkerchief at the same time. The wipers raced back and forth across the windshield.

"Mister Mike, we are playin' who struck John now!"

"Who struck John, what the hell is that supposed to mean?"

"When you are playin' along, and you are just totally improvisin' it up as you go, in the New Orleans jazz world that's called who struck John."

"Yawdy, I don't think I like this song."

We made it along Chartres to Saint Peter Street where we turned towards back o' town until we could make out the outline of the Hall on the left-hand side of the street. The wind was even fiercer than it was at Yawdy's. Blowing over the top of the car, it lifted the wipers completely away from the windshield.

"Yawdy, we'll never get the doors open this way. The wind will tear 'em completely off."

He pointed up the street, "Can you turn around up here at the corner and head back the other way? Bourbon is one way down-rivuh, but I don't think you'll get in trouble tonight."

I pulled on up to Bourbon Street, swung the car around the corner, and smashed into a mammoth trash bin that had blown from somewhere up the street. We backed away from the bin and turned the car enough to clear the edge of the trash container just as the wind blew it around broadside, and into us again.

"Hang on, Yawdy."

I floored the Impala and broke free from the trash bin as it screeched along the side of the car. Something came loose from the side of the bin and shattered the right rear passenger window. We stopped next to the curb in front of 726 Saint Peter Street.

"We get off here, Mr. Rum. Sit tight and let me see if I can get the gate unlocked."

The power must have been off in the entire French Quarter as everything was total darkness, wind, and pounding torrents of rain. The only light came from the reflection of the Impala's headlights into the fury of the storm. Hanging on to the ironwork made opening the lock easier than I expected. The key went into the lock and turned over one full turn. I pushed on the left side of the door and it swung open into the carriage way. I turned around and made a dive for Yawdy's door. I opened it and pushed my back against it to hold it open.

"COME ON, YAWDY," I screamed. "LET ME GET YOU INSIDE, AND THEN I'LL COME BACK FOR THE LUGGAGE."

As I wrapped my arms around him, and we headed for the door, he started singing.

"*Hold that tiger… hold that tiger… hold that tiger…grrrrrrrrrrrrr… and, Mister Mike, Lord don't let him go!*"

TWENTY-TWO

A Fortress

*"He [Satchmo] also taught me by his example,
that the key to music, the key to life, is concentration."*

—Bobby Hackett

I left Yawdy leaning against the wall and out of the wind inside the gate to the carriage way. I made one last dash to the side of the car and knelt down between the car and the curb. The door felt like it weighed five hundred pounds as I pushed it open against the wind. I used the back of my hand to sweep the broken glass from the passenger window off the bags lying on the back seat. I grabbed Yawdy's suitcase and my roller bag and slipped them out behind me next to the car. The rain was coming off the front of the building like someone was standing on top with a fire hose. I stayed on my knees, made my way across the sidewalk back to the gate, and stood up next to Yawdy as I tried to catch my breath. We slammed the wrought iron gate back into place. I felt a sense of security as the latch snapped when the gate was shut.

Just as the heavy gate closed, a rippled piece of heavy curved roofing tin slammed into the Impala at the curb and pierced the windshield. It went in through the front windshield all the way to the back seat with the remainder folding in the wind and wrapping over the top of the car like an opened sardine can. The tin slapped against the roof of the car crashing and banging up and down in the gale. The fury of the hurricane pounded at the Quarter. I'd seen a British Air Force Harrier jet hover over a taxiway at an air show one time in Liberal, Kansas. The deafening howl outside the Hall sounded like we had a dozen jets hovering overhead.

Yawdy yelled, "MISTER MIKE, I'D SAY OUR TIMING IS PRETTY GOOD."

"I THINK IT WOULD HAVE BEEN BETTER IF I WOULD HAVE MADE IT ON A PLANE TO MINNESOTA AND YOU WERE SITTING IN JACKSON WITH ADRIAN," I screamed back at him.

Yawdy tugged at his wet shirt clinging to his chest, "LOOK AT US. MAN, ARE WE A COUPLE OF DROWNED RATS OR WHAT?"

"YAWDY, WE'VE GOT TO GET INTO SOME DRY CLOTHES."

"GRAB YOUR BAG AND FOLLOW ME," he hollered.

Yawdy carried his suitcase and the extra horn case I retrieved from his living room, as he headed to the back of the carriage way and took off up the steps. I grabbed his clarinet case and my roller bag. My briefcase was in the trunk of the Impala where it could stay for all I cared. The screaming from the wind howling through the carriage way diminished as we made our way up the stairs and down a dark interior hallway.

"Yawdy, I can't see a damn thing."

"I'm right in front of you, Mister Mike. Here, come on in this here room."

I stepped through a doorway and stopped. I could hear Yawdy somewhere in front of me. It sounded like he was opening cabinet doors of some sort. Just then, the room flashed from a wooden match he struck in the darkness. He held it up to a cabinet door and opened it to see inside. I could see the bent reflection of the flame on the globe of an old hurricane lamp.

"How appropriate, Mr. Rum."

"Why do you think they call 'em hurricane lamps?"

He set the lamp on the counter, raised the globe, and touched the flame to the wick.

The interior of the room brightened as the flame took hold and he lowered the dusty globe back in place. Within a minute or two, Yawdy had three lamps going that provided a soft glow throughout our fortress. We heard a raspy meow from behind us as Champ made a dash into the room.

"Well, hello fella," Yawdy said to the ol' tomcat. "Bet you were thinkin' you were goin' to have to ride this one out all by yourself."

The old white tomcat sat near the middle of the room blinking his eyes as if not believing he had guests for the occasion. I moved several ratty cardboard boxes off the table sitting in the center of the room, placed Yawdy's old brown suitcase and my roller bag on the table. A fist size bundle of baggage tags hung from the handle of Yawdy's suitcase.

"Yawdy, your suitcase looks like it's been around the world a few times."

"Yes, siree, and there's a story behind every one of those tags, too."

We stripped down, placed our wet clothes on several old wooden chairs and a stainless steel storage rack in the room. While not totally dry, at least we had a change of clothes that were better than the ones we just shed.

Yawdy glanced around the room, "Looks like one of our hotel rooms on the road. Most of the band members never did believe in travelin' with too many clothes. We washed out our skivvies every night and hung 'em up in our rooms."

I looked up at the stained ceiling and walls. "Yawdy, you think we are safe up here, or should we be downstairs?"

"Mister Mike, this old buildin' has been here since 1750. I ain't got no idea how many hurricanes it's seen, but I gotta feelin' we are in one of the best places to be in the whole Crescent City."

The room looked like it doubled for a storage area and kitchen all in one. A double row of tall wooden cabinets with an old yellow countertop ran nearly the full length of the room. A stained porcelain sink with a crook-neck faucet sat at the end of the countertop. Next to the sink stood an old liberty blue Elmira gas stove that looked as if it had cooked many a pot of gumbo, much of it still stuck on the front of the stove. Yawdy rummaged through the cabinets until he recovered two four-inch tall juice glasses. He sat the glasses on the table, leaned over, gave the old cat a couple of pats on the head, and then pulled a pint of Evan Williams from his suitcase.

"Here, I think a night like this calls for a nip."

Yawdy unscrewed the lid and poured each of us a quarter of a glass.

"Now, don't get carried away. Just take your time a sippin' this whiskey. I think we are going to be here for a while."

Yawdy sat down across from me with the glow of the hurricane lamp illuminating his white Fu Manchu. The golden tint of the whiskey in glass was a perfect match for the hue of the room. A huffing wind rattled the hurricane doors on the front of the Hall and tore at the roof above us. I raised my glass and held it next to the fly-speckled lens on the hurricane lamp.

"Mr. Rum, here's to hurricanes. Those we experience from nature and those we create in our own lives. May we learn something from each kind."

Yawdy touched the rim of his glass against mine. We both leaned back as we took a sip of the whiskey. A burning sensation hit the back of my throat and tightened the muscles in my vocal chords.

Yawdy leaned over and picked up the small faded black horn case I retrieved from his living room. He sat it between us on the table. The corners of the horn case were reinforced with rusty metal clasps. The handle had been wrapped with fine piano wire to hold the wooden grip in place. There was a small brass nameplate next to the handle. I rubbed it a bit and noticed the letters B. Bolden.

"What's in there, Yawdy?"

He unlatched the lock and carefully opened the case on the table. Inside was an old cornet. Its condition told a story of years of use.

"B. Bolden. Buddy Bolden?"

"Uh-huh, Mister Mike. You see, I just couldn't let nothin' happen to this old horn."

"This horn belonged to Buddy Bolden?" I asked.

"Yes, it did, the old jazz pappy himself. There aren't any recordins' of Bolden's music. The sounds from this ol' horn are as close as you can get to the roots of jazz. Kinda like goin' back to the dawn of life itself."

Yawdy carefully removed the cornet from the case. He tapped the mouthpiece into place and raised the horn to his lips. He started slowly at first. It was like he was savoring that horn as much as the whiskey. He began playing a simple riff that led into "Swing Low, Sweet Chariot." After a couple of choruses he lowered the horn and looked across the table at me.

"Do you know where I got this ol' horn?"

"Did you find it here in the Hall?"

"Nope. Your Great-uncle Amos won it in a poker game."

"You're kiddin'? You bought it from him?"

"Nope. He gave it to me. He said he didn't need no horn, said he wouldn't even know how to take care of it, and that I should have it."

"Holy cow, Yawdy, my great-uncle gave you that horn. What are the odds?"

"Yeah, somethin' ain't it? Life's full of strange connections."

He put the horn back to his lips and, for what seemed like an eternity, rolled from one song to another, announcing the title and providing a bit of background info for each one–"Ain't Misbehavin," "Down by the Riverside," "Somebody Else is Taking My Place," "His Eye is On the Sparrow," "After Hours," "Heebie Jeebies," "I Believe I Can Make It By Myself," and "What Am I Here For." All the while, his right foot kept a steady tapping on the old wooden floor.

"Yawdy, a private concert, I'm honored."

I raised the juice glass and took another sip of the whiskey. This time it was smoother.

"If I didn't know better, I'd say you picked those out for a reason."

Yawdy laid the horn back across the case and took a sip from his glass.

"Well, I guess I just had a certain feelin'."

"And that would be?" I asked.

"I'm feelin' this ain't the only hurricane we got to deal with. I'm thinkin' you got one goin' on in your life, too."

"Yeah, I hit my own hurricane. That sucker got me right between the eyes, splat!"

"What's up?"

"I was over in Lafayette this week for a quick meeting and a performance review with my boss. We've been having a hard time coordinating schedules, so we just did it there."

"And?"

"Well, after I was down here last time and I told you what happened on that trip to Kansas, I went back home and decided I ought to send a short letter of apology to Harry."

"And?"

"I sent it and told him that I didn't want him to misconstrue my passion for the salt business with arrogance. That I had spent several years on the production side of the business and felt a special appreciation for what went on at the plant level. And that if I had insulted him in any way, I was sorry."

"How'd he respond?"

"He never did. He gave the letter to my boss. Long story short, my boss threw the letter in my face and said I stabbed him in the back. He said he got the letter from Harry."

"Stabbed him in the back, with an apology letter?"

"That's what he said."

Yawdy's eyes opened wide as he said, "That ol' boy is even more scared than I thought he might be. Folks react in weird ways when they're scared."

"He claimed, in addition to the letter, I was undermining his direction for the business and I needed to go."

"Did you get fired?"

"No. That really doesn't happen at my level. They are willing to make it worth my time to leave."

"Sounds like bein' fired to me."

"I've got some time to make the decision if I really want to leave."

"But he wants you gone right?"

"Right."

"So you really don't have no choice but to go?"

"I'd say you're probably right."

"Probably, hell, man, they want you out of their hair."

"Well, Yawdy, let's put it in perspective. I'm feeling there comes a point when your goals and aspirations for your life don't match up with what you're doing."

"So you feel like there's a need for a change as much as your boss does," Yawdy offered. "And it's not an option to stay where you are, 'cause you are catchin' too much heat for being a free spirit," he added.

"Yes."

"Mister Mike, do you think this only affects you or other folks as well?"

"I believe there are a lot of people that struggle with similar issues, maybe just in a different part of their life."

Yawdy leaned a bit forward over the table. "Every day folks find themselves in situations they would like to change. Sometimes somethin' happens that makes you aware of the need for a change in your life, and sometimes the need for a change is forced on you."

"I suppose no matter who or where you are in life," I added.

"No matter nothin'—no matter if you're young or old, no matter if you're man or a woman, no matter if you're rich or poor, no matter you're if black or white. It's all 'bout payin' attention to what's goin' on in your life and thinkin' 'bout what needs changin'."

I leaned back on my chair as I tried to comprehend what he was saying. Yawdy was on a roll. His passion was coming through; his eyes ignited with fiery conviction.

"Does it matter whether a change is forced on you or you chose it of your own volition?" I asked.

"A person might be better off if they can come to the realization all on their own, but even if the need for a change is forced on 'em some folks still don't change. I think it starts with bein' fully aware of what's goin' on in your life and about what you need to change in order to grow. Then after you're aware of what you need to change, you gotta get at it."

"Get at it, you mean work on the change?"

"I sure do. Mister Mike, you said you aren't fittin' in the mold you need to in order to stay with the company, that right?"

"Yes."

"You see, for some folks, what needs changin' might not be how they perform in their job. It could be in a totally different area. It might be a family relationship—bein' a better husband or wife, or mom, or a pop, or brother, or sister, bein' a better aunt, or an uncle. Maybe it's about doin' more in your church or community. Could even be about somethin' you might like to learn about or be able to do. It could even be a health issue that needs attention."

I looked Yawdy square in those big brown eyes, "Maybe even like taking their medicine when they're supposed to, like someone I know."

A wide grin spread across Yawdy's face, "why, yes siree. I'm a perfect example. I had somethin' goin' on with my ol'prostate gland. And, you know even after I had some minor surgery I still wasn't payin' attention to it. But, let me tell you, after that last bout, it sure as hell got my attention. I've changed, and I'm a takin' my medicine. You never get too old to make changes in your life. Mister Mike, sounds like to me, you have some thinkin' to do about your changes and that book you told me you want to write."

"Like thinking if I'm really serious or not?"

"You're the only one that knows the answer to that question. From what you've told me you've already been movin' in the direction you want to take your life."

"Yawdy, you've hinted at a secret. Something we already know, but don't know. Something we've heard a thousand times, but never really heard. Something that is so profound, it can change our life. What the hell is it?"

"Mister Mike, I think you're ready. You kinda got yourself in your own hurricane. That's what happens when you don't pay attention to what's goin' on. Everythin' goes to hell in a hand basket, and then a guy loses his options. Kinda like us here this mornin'. Ol' Yawdy's secret begins with payin' attention."

I blinked my eyes a few times, trying to get a grip on what he just said. "Paying attention. You mean just paying attention?"

"No, not just payin' attention. I mean really payin' attention. You see, that day you was travelin' with those bigwigs, well, you just wasn't payin' attention. With your boss, you haven't been payin' attention."

"Paying attention," I said again, as I tried to make sure I understood the full context of what he had just said. Surely, it had to be more complex than that.

"When you start payin' attention, life takes on new meanin'. If'n you want to harmonize your life, there is only one way to do it."

Yawdy poured each of us another shot of the Evan Williams. I sat looking into the complexities of Yawdy's aging face.

"Yawdy, how can it be that simple?"

"It ain't simple. It's the hardest damn thin' to do in the world. Just look around. You'll see people in all walks of life who aren't payin' attention. Just pick somethin'."

"How about our relationships with others?"

"If you are in an unhappy relationship, you gotta start payin' attention. What's at the root of it? What's causin' the festerin'? You gotta listen, you gotta use that head on your shoulders for what the Ol' Boy upstairs gave it to you for."

"And if it's the other person?"

"A lot of times it's not the other person. Oh, we want to think it is. Hell, that's the easy excuse—it ain't my fault. Fact of the matter is, about 99 percent of the time, it is our fault. We are squarely to blame for the lack of harmony in our relationships with others."

"But if you change and things don't get better, then what?"

"You're still gonna learn somethin' in the process."

"Okay. Let's say someone's in a relationship with a person who's an alcoholic. How does paying attention help there?"

"If you start payin' attention, you might find you were empowerin' that other person to keep drinkin'. This ain't about molly coddlin'. It's about gettin' at the root of things, both for yourself and the important people in your life."

"And if you are the one doing the drinking?"

"If you happen to be the one doin' the drinkin', and you can't be reasonable about it, then you gotta pay attention and stop."

"But some people can't do that."

"Then you gotta pay attention and get help. If'n you can't control it, you gotta do whatever it takes in order to not take that next drink."

"How about smoking?"

"You see, if you really start payin' attention, you'll stop smokin'. If you slow down, and listen to your body, and what havin' a cough or bein' out of breath or always havin' sinus problems is tellin' you; you'll quit. It won't be easy, but you'll do it. Mister Mike, you told me you used to smoke. You stopped. How did you do it?"

"Started running, focused on how I felt, and found I couldn't do both."

"You paid attention, and you changed. So did I."

Champ jumped up on Yawdy's lap and nuzzled his head under Yawdy's hand on the edge of the table. Yawdy looked down and began rubbing the old cat's ears.

"I suppose you'd say the obesity problem in this country today is a result of people not paying attention," I offered.

"For sure. You think one day all of a sudden you go to your closet, and somebody shrunk your pants? No way, man, those extra pounds creep up on you, and if you ain't payin' attention, pretty soon you're buyin' bigger clothes just to have somethin' to put on. If you keep it up, and don't pay attention to the signs, pretty soon you've got big-time health problems—high blood pressure, heart problems, diabetes, and all kinds of bad stuff. It may take a few years, but it will finally catch up with you. Hell, I'd call it a health hurricane."

"But some people won't admit they've got a problem; they deny it."

"Some folks has got to go all the way to the bottom before they get to a point they are ready to pay attention. And, I'll admit, sadly enough, lots of folks don't make it."

"Yawdy, do you think this works for every aspect of our lives?"

"Mister Mike, in all my years, I ain't never seen no place that payin' attention don't work. When you start payin' attention, and I mean really payin' attention, you can harmonize every aspect of your life."

"Do you know how many times in our lives someone told us we needed to pay attention?"

He shrugged his shoulders. "A thousand, a hundred thousand, heck, maybe a million times."

"A million is probably close. Do you think that's why we don't do it, because we've heard it so much we're deaf to the instructions to pay attention?"

"Could be. In all likelihood someone's been tellin' us to pay attention since we were barely old enough to take notice," he offered as he took a deep breath and swung his legs around to one side of his chair and placed the contented cat down on the floor.

"Yawdy, we need something to break through the fog, something that could help us pay attention to what's going on in our lives before we get caught up in our own self-generated hurricanes. Not something that allows us to pay attention only to one single area, but something that lets us make meaningful progress with the whole person. What's the answer?"

He stood up, carefully lifted one of the flickering hurricane lamps off the cabinet, and walked to the door leading to the hallway.

"One step at a time," he said as he turned and walked down the hallway. "One step at a…"

TWENTY-THREE

The Wisdom of Yawdy Rum

"Bring the good old bugle boy!
We'll sing another song.
Sing it with spirit that will start the world along."

—Henry Clay

I stood at the end of the hallway on the second floor leaning against the stairway handrail waiting for Yawdy to come back up from the carriage way. Heavy rain swept across a row of wooden framed windows along the back side of the old building. It came in sheets and distorted the view through the windows against the dark sky. Intermittent flashes of lightning highlighted what remained of the leaves on the trees whipping back and forth inside the courtyard. The wind outside maintained a constant, eerie moan. I wondered what was happening to the city. The old fellow on the *Creole Queen* talked about the city's flood control pumps. I sure as hell hoped they were working. *And how about the old riverboat, was she holding her own against the onslaught?* I was so carried away in thought, I hadn't noticed Yawdy standing next to me at the top of the stairs.

"Still gettin' with it out there," he said, as he stared along with me out into the dark fury.

"No kidding," I answered. "What time is it?"

He handed me the hurricane lamp he carried as he pulled his shirt sleeve up to expose his watch. The dark skin on the back of his hand looked tanned and leathery.

"I got about 6:30 a.m. Sure dark, ain't it?"

"Boy, I'll say. How long does a hurricane last, Yawdy?"

"Hard to tell. If this ol' storm is as big as they say, I'd estimate we got several hours of blowin' left. Could be late this afternoon by the time it lets up."

"How do you think the city is doing?"

"I don't know, Mister Mike. She's seen a bunch of 'em over the years. But it's certainly tearin' up Ned out there right now."

"Tearing up Ned. I swear, Yawdy, you've got more dang expressions. Is tearing up Ned anything like playing who struck John?"

"Worse. You want a bite to eat?"

"What do you have?"

"Royal Crown brand spicy sardines and Nabisco soda crackers."

"I guess beggars can't be choosers. Lead the way."

I followed Yawdy back into the old musty room that had become our makeshift home. The hurricane lamps actually made it feel quite cozy. Champ had curled up in Yawdy's suitcase he'd left open on the floor. He seemed to have little concern for what was going on outside. Yawdy put out a couple of small yellow paper plates he found in one of the cabinets and opened a box of soda crackers. The sardines let out a rush of fishy gas as he opened the can. The aroma of mustard and hot sauce filled the room and brought the cat out of his slumber. Yawdy put four soda crackers on his plate and handed the package to me. He used a plastic fork to catch a couple of the glistening oily fish and place them onto a cracker. He put another cracker squarely on top and made a sandwich out of it. He took a careful bite, and while still chewing on the morsels cleared his throat, and continued our discussion.

"Mister Mike, what did you ask me before we headed downstairs?"

"What's the trick to paying attention?"

Yawdy leaned back in his chair, and put his feet up on the edge of the table. "No trick to it, just a matter of thinkin' seriously about where you are and where you really want to be. Let's go back to eatin'. Let's say I ain't been payin' attention and I find myself in the doctor's office for some reason. I step up on his scales and they tell me I weigh three hundred pounds. I look at the doctor, and he says, 'Why, Mister Yawdy Rum, how you doin'?' And my answer is, 'Oh, doc, I'm doin' pretty good.' Pretty good my butt. I ain't doin' good at all. I'm lyin' to myself. I'm not payin' attention and chances are I haven't been payin' attention for quite a while. Any health problems I'm likely to have are squarely my fault, ain't no one else can take the blame."

"So, Yawdy, are you saying I wasn't paying attention to the things I needed to at work and everything that's happened is my fault?"

"Maybe."

"Maybe?" I asked.

It took me a bit, but I finally caught one of the sardines swimming in the bright red sea of oil and laid it across the cracker. It didn't smell any better than it looked. One quick swallow and it felt like it was still trying to swim back upstream. A little sip of the whiskey helped wash it on along.

Yawdy looked squarely at me and said, "You been tellin' me you've always wanted to write a book, but you couldn't do it with all the demands on your time. You told me that you didn't plan to work in the salt mines forever anyway."

"Yes."

"I asked you about money, and you said you could go along for a while until you could get somethin' goin' on your own."

"Yes."

"Now, it sounds like to me you got a better deal."

"Better deal?"

"Sounds like indirectly they are willin' to pay you to get that book written. Now, Mister Mike, everyone doesn't want the same as you. Some folks would be glad just to have a good job, and that's okay 'cause we all got a different definition of what success looks like."

"But what are you saying?"

"I'm sayin', if you got an itch to do somethin' in your life and you don't do it, you will have cheated yourself, and everyone else in the process, especially the Maker that put you here."

"Yawdy, I hear you saying we need to pay attention to that inner voice."

"Mmmm hmmm, that's it."

"You think everyone has that voice?"

"Yep. Unless maybe you are mentally ill, and then I'll bet you still have it, you just don't understand it."

"Okay. So let's say I agree with you, that it all comes down to paying attention. What's the secret to doing it not once, but every day?"

Yawdy got up from the table and walked over to the row of cabinets. He opened a couple of doors before he reached in and produced a blank sheet of staff paper. Then he opened the drawer next to the sink and retrieved a short, stubby yellow pencil before returning to his chair.

"Mister Mike, people almost never start payin' attention until somethin' happens in their life to shake things up a bit. Then, dependin' on how serious it is, and sometimes even that don't matter, they may or may not change."

Yawdy stuck out his tongue, licked the end of the short little pencil, and he wrote across the top of the page: Yawdy's Wisdom. Then he numbered one through seven down the side of the page with Roman numerals.

This was it. This was his secret. This was going to be a list of what he had discovered in life that would bring harmony and growth. I wasn't sure I was ready to hear what he was going to tell me. Somehow the suspense of wondering about the old man's secret was one thing, but now that he was about to fully disclose it, I wondered if I was ready to hear it. And once I did, what was it going to mean for my life? It was like he was harnessing the fury of the hurricane and driving the energy of it onto the page sitting on the table in front of me.

He began, "**I: Largo**. It means to play slowly. You can't improve what's goin' on in your life if you're always racin' around. You gotta slow down, and I mean way slow. When you are tryin' to learn a piece of music and all you can do is make mistakes, the only way to improve is to play so slowly you can watch your hands and listen to every single note. Then, and only then, can you adjust and improve. That's what I tried to show you the very first time we played together in my livin' room. Shoot, now-a-days folks are runnin' around goin' ninety miles an hour all the time. Between computers, cell phones, and all kinds of instant messagin' gadgets, there ain't never time to go slow and think about what's goin' on in your life. Goin' slow allows you to pay closer attention and make improvement. You gotta go slow to understand what needs changin'. Otherwise you just keep on makin' all the mistakes today you made yesterday."

He continued, "**II: D.C. al Fine**. Dal capo, the head. al Fine, to the end. From the beginnin' to the end. To improve, it's all about goin' back to the beginnin' and playin' it through step by step, playin' it through completely in your mind. You gotta think about everythin' that's goin' on, what's right, what's wrong, what's workin', what's not, and why. And you gotta be critical in your review. You can't go sugar coatin' any of it. You gotta be honest with yourself. Understandin' what you need to do to make improvements in your life will only come to you when you reflect back in your thinkin'. You have to be totally honest with yourself about how you got to where you are, and what you need to do to change."

"Yawdy, you've mentioned this to me on more than one occasion when we've been together. I didn't really catch the full importance of it until now. I wasn't paying attention."

"I told you, Mister Mike, all this ain't easy. Nothin' in life of value ever is." He continued, "**III: Dynamics & Tempo**. Dynamics and Tempo are the signposts in sheet music that tell you to play louder, softer, faster, or slower. I told you the first time we played together at my place how dynamics and tempo are like our five senses. Our senses act as signposts in our lives, but we gotta listen to 'em. What're our senses tellin' us? Where's the harmony and the disharmony? You see, Mister Mike, our senses are our tools for understandin' what's happenin' in our lives. That's why the Creator gave 'em to us. Payin' attention to our senses and listenin' to what they are sayin' to us is critical."

"You're talking about sight, sound, taste, touch, and smell, right?"

"Mmmm-huh. They are the only ones I'm 100 percent sure of. But, sometimes there is somethin' more. A feelin' we get about how we're doin', whether we're makin' any progress or not. People receive all the information they need to be successful, if they'll only pay attention to the dynamics and tempo of their lives. Each and every one of the relationships in our lives has its own dynamics and tempo as well. To be successful we've got to pay attention to the information comin' at us. If you were to try and play the "Saints", and you gave no attention to the dynamics and tempo, there certainly wouldn't be no marchin' goin' on."

"I'm following you."

"If you want to be successful, if you want to be happy in this life, you have to learn to listen to your senses. Ignore them and you'll suffer the consequences."

The flame in the hurricane globe bent slightly as Yawdy moved the lamp a couple of inches to the side in order for him to position the full sheet of paper on the wooden table.

"**IV: The Score**. You gotta write down what a successful outcome looks like, you gotta get it on paper."

"Yawdy, you told me to do that the day we met in Louis Armstrong Park."

"Yeah, I did. Have you done it?'

"Yes. I've written out each of my goals in an outline form and captured the most important aspects of what I'd like to achieve."

Yawdy's brown eyes studied the stubby little yellow pencil, "How you do it all depends on your personal preference. The important thing is to get it written down in a manner in which it means somethin' to you. A musician would never know for sure if they were playin' a song like the composer meant it to be played if'n they didn't have the musical notation to follow. How much you actually write down depends on your own style. Some folks need to write out more than others in order to have a clear picture of what success looks like. The main thing is you gotta get it out of your head and get it written down on a piece of paper. "

"Okay, that makes sense."

"Ol' Yawdy always makes sense. **V: Repeat**. You have to repeat the desired behavior enough times to make it rote. You can't just do it once or twice and then go off thinkin' you got it mastered. The only way you can improve is through daily practice. You show me a musician who don't never practice and I'll show you someone who's not a musician."

"You're saying repetition reinforces the right actions," I clarified.

"Yep, and the right thinkin', too. I told you that day you were at my place and we were playin' that sweet Gibson guitar the repeat symbol was one of the most practical tools in written music. I told you it works for your life in the same manner."

"How many times do you think we have to repeat the right actions in order to improve?"

"I'll give you a rule of thumb I got from ol' Furst Manassas; 'member me talkin' about him?"

"Yep. He was your clarinet teacher when you were a kid."

"He'd say, 'Yawdy, boy, you play that riff perfect at least five times, and you got it.'"

"Five times, that's all?" I asked.

"No, not just five times, five times exactly perfect all in a row. Achieving exactly the outcome you are lookin' for. Not almost perfect, not nearly perfect, perfect. PERFECT!"

"Are you saying I can't improve unless I can do something absolutely perfect?"

"Of course not. Life is as much about the journey as it is the destination. Improvement often happens in little steps over time. The key is to be repeatin' the right actions and behaviors in our relationship with ourselves and others. Are you ready for number six?"

"Sure, keep going."

"**VI: Rest**. Whether it's a piece of music or your life, takin' time to rest is critical. Time to breathe, time to refresh. Rest is about pausin'. The rests in a song add to the rhythm along with the notes. Restin' gives you energy. If you're always goin' along at full speed, and you never take time to rest, you'll burn out. You'll lose your sense of appreciation for the richness and beauty of life. In a New Orleans jazz band the solos give the other musicians a bit of time to rest, catch their breath, and to regenerate for a few moments before pickin' up their part again."

"Yawdy, I'm not sure we give ourselves permission to rest in today's world."

"Ain't nobody able to answer that question 'cept yourself. I also think the amount of rest needed varies from one person to the next.

But I know one thing for certain, can't nobody go without it and still be successful."

"So rest probably has a more individual aspect to it," I added.

"Yep. **VII: Believe in yourself and don't hesitate to ask the Bandleader for help**."

"Bandleader? Are you referring to God?"

"I'm referrin' to whoever you think the Bandleader might be for you. Some folks might call that God; some say Universal Law; others the Budda, Mohammed, Christ, or even the Great Spirit."

"Pray?" I asked.

"I always have been a believer in askin' a Higher Power for some help when you are tryin' to improve things in your life. Ain't no sense in you carryin' the load all by yourself."

Yawdy finished writing number seven on the paper then pushed it across the table to me. He centered the flickering hurricane lamp on the table and laid the pencil next to it. "There you go, Mister Mike. Ol' Yawdy's secret—Yawdy's wisdom on payin' attention. Payin' attention to harmonize every aspect of your life, because when you finally start payin' attention you can discover the courage to change."

YAWDY's WISDOM

I . LARGO. Slow down, So you can pay attention.

II. D.C. AL FINE. Go back to the beginning. Play it through in your mind. THINK.

III. DYNAMICS + TEMPO. Pay attention to your senses.

IV. THE SCORE. Write out a description of a successful outcome.

V. REPEAT. Repeat goal centered actions + behaviors.

VI. REST. Take time to rest.

VII. BELIEVE IN YOURSELF. + don't hesitate to ask the Bandleader for Help.

"Now that you ain't got a job and you need somethin' to do, you take ol' Yawdy's wisdom and go to work."

I stared over the top of the old hurricane lamp sitting between us and peered deeply into the glow on Yawdy's face, observing the deep, wide furrowed lines across his brow, and into those big round sparkling brown eyes. He was entrusting me with something he considered to be extremely valuable.

"So my Great-uncle Amos won that horn in a poker game?"

"Ain't it sweet?"

"Yes, it is, Yawdy. Yes, it is."

My cell phone broke the silence. I had clipped it to my belt hanging over the metal rack behind us. I jumped up and grabbed the phone from the clip. Caller ID showed it was Grantland calling.

"Hello, Mike, I figured you were stuck somewhere after I talked with your wife on the phone. She said you and your old jazz buddy were either at the mine or more likely still in New Orleans, and you could probably use any help you could get," Grantland offered with a bit of a chuckle.

"We're not stuck; we're just waiting it out. I can't believe you got through on my cell phone. I've been getting a busy signal every time I've tried to use it."

"Just lucky, I guess. Is everything okay?"

"Well, it's just the two of us, and we are in one piece. That's probably more than you can say for the Crescent City and what's left of our rental car, if it's still outside. It took a direct hit last night with somebody's roof. How about you?"

"I think most places west of New Orleans are coming through the storm just fine, but I'm hearing they are concerned about the levees in and around the city. If you want to get out, I'll try to get over there and pick you up this afternoon. But we don't have time for you to think about it. When the storm breaks we're going to have to make a quick run at it."

I looked over at Yawdy. He was rolling his tongue around inside that wide jaw of his chasing out another sardine.

"You up for a ticket out of here, Mr. Rum?"

"I think that'd be swell. Jackson would be a nice place to be for a few days if you're lookin' for a place for us to hole up."

I put the cell phone back to my ear. "Grantland, can you please call my wife and let her know we're okay?"

"Be glad to," he answered.

"We're at Preservation Hall at 726 Saint Peter Street. Do you think you can get us to Jackson?"

"I'll head that way as soon as the storm breaks. I'm thinking I can make it around 6:00 p.m. or so."

"We'll be ready."

"Mike, if I can't get down into the Quarter, you may have to walk out to I-10 to meet me. Are you and your old friend up for it?"

"We'll do whatever it takes to hook up with you."

I closed the cell phone and placed it on the table. I picked up the sheet of paper on which Yawdy had been writing. I looked at the list of seven items and the words he had written. "Yawdy, I don't know what to say."

"No need to say a thing, Mister Mike. No need to say a thing."

TWENTY-FOUR

The New, New Orleans

"Jazz is a symbol of the triumph of the human spirit."

—Archie Shepps

Three months later

A stiff fall breeze billowed my jacket as Patrick and I walked along the sidewalk framed by the black iron fence on the river side of Jackson Square. Shoulder-to-shoulder my same height, he stayed relatively close to my side as we made our way through the Quarter. His blonde hair fluttered back and forth in the wind. It was Thanksgiving break, and since I was out of the corporate rat race and had no set schedule to maintain, Sharon and I had decided it might be good to have him make the trip to New Orleans with me.

A group of national guard soldiers in a squatty Humvee gave a thumbs up as they rumbled past us on Decatur. The desert sand-colored four-wheeler left behind a trail of sooty diesel fumes as it rumbled up the street. Considering all the damage we'd seen around the city the past couple of days, it looked like they'd be needed for some time to come to help put New Orleans back in order. The haunting images of rusty brown flooded-out homes and businesses in the ninth ward were frozen in my mind. The bright orange numbers and symbols spray-painted on the building fronts gave an eerie reminder of what had been discovered inside–two cats on one, one dog on another, three birds, two elderly, and on more than a dozen homes we'd seen, the number of fatalities. We stopped at a crosswalk on the north side of Decatur and Saint Ann Streets as we waited for the light to change. A young police officer standing on the corner, sharply dressed in a crisp blue uniform, looked our way and smiled.

"W'lcome to Nawlins'," he said. "First trip?"

"No, actually I've been here many times."

"Both of you?" He looked at Patrick.

"Oh, no, this is his first time. I think it's a lot for him to take in."

"Well, it's a different city today. We've got a lot of rebuilding to do. The good news is the Quarter is in pretty good shape. Some of the neighborhoods are really a sad sight, though."

"New Orleans is more than the Quarter," I offered. "It's the people and the culture. That's what seems to be missing."

"It'll take some time, but she's a great ol' city. We'll pick her up and put her back together."

Patrick tugged on my coat sleeve. He'd noticed the light had turned. We stepped off the curb and trotted across the street to Café Du Monde. The patio was filling with morning patrons feasting on fresh beignets and coffee.

"Dad, something smells good."

"Hang on, buddy, you're in for a treat."

I gave the tables in the patio area a quick scan, but didn't see who we were looking for. A lanky, straight-faced waiter wearing glasses with thin bright blue frames stood just inside the tall white arched French doors to the main restaurant. He pushed one of the doors aside and invited us in.

"Good morning, gentlemen, welcome to Café Du Monde. May I seat you at a table?"

I made eye contact across the dining room. "No, thanks, we'll join those folks next to the window."

Yawdy, wearing his familiar black beret with a left-leaning tilt was already standing by the time we reached his table.

"It's great to see you, Mr. Rum." My arms encircled the old man, and I felt him lean into me as I stepped close. His white whiskers tickled the side of my face. Adrian, with her hair tied back with a fiery red bandana, stepped around from the back side of the table and joined the embrace. "Hi, Adrian, you both look great. I've got someone I'd like you to meet." I swung around, placed my hand on Patrick's left shoulder and introduced him to Yawdy and Adrian. They both shook his hand then Yawdy stepped back, pulled out a chair for Patrick, and invited us to sit down. The morning sunlight filtered through the steamy windows along the front of the café and gave a misty white overcast to the room. As I pulled out my chair, Yawdy looked past me to the tall, lanky waiter with coal black hair and funky glasses who stepped up behind us.

"Looks like your party is here. What can I get for you, Mister Yawdy?" he asked.

"Black coffees and a double order," he stopped in mid-sentence. "No, make it a triple. I'm thinkin' this long-legged Minnesota boy can get an order down all by himself." Yawdy rested his hand on Patrick's shoulder. "Mister Patrick, is you a coffee drinker, or would you like some hot chocolate?"

Patrick gave me a quick glance and said, "Hot chocolate, Dad."

I motioned toward Yawdy. "You need to say that to Mr. Rum."

He turned slowly, didn't quite make eye contact with Yawdy, and said, "Hot chocolate, please."

Yawdy looked up at the solemn waiter waiting for us to confirm our order.

"Make it a triple order, a hot chocolate, and three black coffees."

"I couldn't imagine the Quarter without Café Du Monde," I said.

"No, it's certainly a treasure," Yawdy replied. "Where are you staying?"

"We're at the Saint Marie. They're back open."

Yawdy pointed outside the front windows, "Lots of things are comin' back to life, but man, oh, man, is there a lot of work to be done. The ol' Crescent girl has lost part of her soul. She may never fully regain it. Many folks are talkin' about the loss and how the storm was all bad, but it may not be that way at all. It may be some Higher Power scatterin' the beauty and essence of this place all across the country," Yawdy explained.

"How long have you two been back in the Quarter?" I asked.

Adrian spoke first. "About a month."

"Not long enough," Yawdy added.

"Patrick and I were by your place yesterday, Yawdy. It looks in pretty good shape. How about yours, Adrian?"

Her button brown eyes squinted as she answered, "A little problem with the roof, but other than that my place is fine. I think the Quarter was the driest place in town. We are so very lucky. So many, many people lost everything, and not just here, it's a mess nearly all the way to Mobile.

Yawdy spoke up, "It's a little nicer out there today than the last time you were here, and we tried to drive that beat-up rental car out of the Quarter."

I winked at Yawdy, "Yeah, and we thought it was going to be so easy."

Yawdy leaned toward Patrick just a bit and said, "Talk about a couple of fools, your Dad and I thought we'd head out of the city like it was a Sunday afternoon drive."

I looked at Yawdy, "Didn't work, did it?"

"Nope. We ended up stayin' at the Hall four nights." Yawdy leaned even closer to Patrick. "Patrick, ask your Dad if he's ever going to eat any more sardines."

Patrick looked at me but didn't say a word.

"Patrick, you tell Mr. Yawdy Rum he can have all the sardines in the world for all I care. Living off them for four days was enough for me in one lifetime."

"But I still don't understand how you were able to drive out of the Quarter when so many others were stranded," Adrian asked.

"Guess, we just hit it lucky. What was it, Yawdy, about noon on Thursday when we finally got the car in a shape we could drive it? The good part was the Quarter stayed high and dry."

The waiter returned with our steaming coffees, Patrick's hot chocolate, and three orders of glistening white mountains of beignets, the treasures of Du Monde.

"Need anything else, just holler," he remarked as he turned and headed back towards the kitchen.

"We will. Thank you, sir," Adrian responded softly.

Yawdy picked up a plate of pure beignet delight and placed it directly in front of Patrick. "There you go, Son, get after 'em."

In a heartbeat we were all enveloped in the clinging, dusty powdered sugar. The coffee provided the necessary lubricant to wash it down. Patrick didn't say a word. He simply raised his eyebrows, opened his bright blue eyes wide, and dived into the sugary delight.

Yawdy continued, "We used Johnny's ball bat from the carriage way to knock out the rest of the glass that hadn't been broken out by the sheet of curved roofing that was stuck in through the car. It was the first time in my life I ever rode in a new car without no windshield."

"My friend Grantland from over in Lafayette couldn't make it into the Quarter because the police had blocked off all incoming traffic, so we figured we could drive the rental car out to meet him on I-10. What a hoot. Once your uncle and I pulled out the sheet metal that was stuck through the windshield, we had some options."

Yawdy jumped in. "'Cept we only had half a steering wheel, no windshield, soaking wet seats, and only a piece of the gearshift lever."

Patrick hadn't even drawn a breath of air. He was all into the beignets.

"On our way out of the Quarter, we drove through water over to Camp Street where we circled around and got up on highway 90, and out to I-10. We thought it might be too deep, but we made it."

"I still can't believe what you two did with the car," Adrian commented.

Yawdy looked across the table at me as I said, "It was your idea and a fine one at that."

Yawdy turned to Patrick, "Your dad and I gave away that beat up ol' rental car. There was this lady walkin' along the side of Williams Street out by the airport where we hooked up with your dad's buddy from Lafayette. She had five scared little kids with her tryin' to get out of the city. We figured she needed the car more than we did. The last time we saw her, she had all those kids tucked down on the floorboard, and she was headed west on 1-10. She said it was the nicest car she'd ever driven, that she had a sister in Houston, and she wasn't goin' to stop till she got there."

"I still don't understand how you explained that to the rental car company." Adrian commented.

"Well, Adrian," I said, "we figured she needed that car more than National did, and it was probably only one of many they wrote off the books due to the hurricane."

"But what did you tell them?" she asked.

"They never asked."

"Do you think she made it?"

Yawdy spoke up, "With the determination in that woman's eyes, I think she could have driven all the way to California, if she would have had too. Unless she was too windblown by the time she got to Texas, ha."

"I swear, you two are a couple of lucky bums," Adrian remarked as she took a sip of her coffee.

I reached into my pants pocket and removed the shiny little guitar charm she had sold, and laid it on the table. "Maybe it was the gris-gris."

She picked up the charm, smiled wide, and held it in her hand before she laid it back on the table. A clown appeared outside the window on the sidewalk. He was forming some type of object out of a long skinny, bright red balloon. Adrian leaned over closer to Patrick.

"Patrick, wanna go out and check him out with me?" she asked.

Patrick quickly looked at me, as if he wasn't sure he should leave me at the table with Yawdy. "It's okay, you can go." He stood up from the table, followed Adrian across the room, and out the tall arched French doors. I finished the coffee that was in my cup and took one last bite from the beignet on the small china plate in front of me.

"How's it going for you, Mister Mike?" Yawdy asked.

"Well, I'm off and running, Yawdy. I've been spending all my time on the research and initial writing for the book. The wisdom you shared is timeless. I feel I owe you so much. I don't know how I'll ever pay you back for what you've shared with me."

"Hey, you're the one doin' all the work."

"That might be true, but the idea came from you."

"Well, let's just hope there are people who will read the words written in your book, will really think about payin' attention to what's goin' on in their lives, and apply a bit of ol' Yawdy's wisdom to make things better. Even if somewhere just one person makes a positive change, that's payback enough for both of us, Mister Mike."

"I hope it's more than one person, Yawdy. I hope everyone who reads the book will find a way to apply your wisdom in order to find a greater level of success and happiness in their lives."

"And the salt business?"

"That's part of my past now."

"Miss'n it?" he asked.

"Just the friends I had in the business."

Yawdy and I sat chatting for several minutes. It was fun to reconnect with him. He told me what he planned to do over the next few months. He explained how he wanted to help the city get going again, and how he felt he could make a difference.

Adrian and Patrick returned from outside and joined us back at the table. Patrick carried a brightly colored array of twisted balloons. They squeaked as he displayed the creation to Yawdy and me.

"It's a flower pot, Dad. I'll take it home to Mom."

Yawdy made eye contact with Patrick. "Mister Patrick, your dad tells me you're nearly finished with school. What are you goin' to do when you're done?"

"Uh-uh. I'm moving to Florida," Patrick answered.

"Florida," Yawdy responded with a puzzled look. "What are you goin' to do there?"

"Move in with my brother."

I winked at Yawdy.

"What's he think about that?" Yawdy asked.

Patrick shifted his glance from the single beignet left on his plate, up to me, and quickly back again.

I interrupted, "I'm not sure his brother knows anything about it at this point."

When you are autistic, you think anything that's in your mind, is also known to everyone else in the same manner. Patrick dove into the last beignet.

"So how long will you be here?" Adrian asked.

"We are headed home tomorrow. I think the research for the book is pretty much completed."

"What's the timeline for your book, Mike?"

"That all depends on the editor and the publishing process."

Yawdy piped up, "Remember, you promised ol' Yawdy the first copy."

"I wouldn't have it any other way, Mr. Rum. It's your secret. I'm only the messenger."

"We all have a different position to play in the band. It takes each one to make it all work," he added.

"It takes folks like you, Yawdy Rum, to share their gifts with the world. It makes it a better place for all of us. By the way, Yawdy, what was the final number for the horn?"

"What do you mean?" he asked.

"The benefit auction on e-Bay that was held for the hurricane victims," I clarified. "I know you donated an old cornet that belonged to a 'B. Bolden'. Did I hear the final bid correctly?" I asked.

Adrian reached across the table and placed her hand on top of her uncle's.

"Three million bucks, Mister Mike, and all of it going back to the folks in New Orleans tryin' to rebuild their lives."

"Wow, Yawdy, that's great, but I'll bet you'll miss noodling around on that old horn."

"Not really."

"Not really, I thought you loved that instrument."

"I did," Yawdy added. "But it's no big deal."

"No big deal, what do you mean?" I asked.

"Your great-uncle won two horns in that poker game."

BOOK CLUB DISCUSSION GUIDE

1. The main character in *The Wisdom of Yawdy Rum* struggles to balance his work life with his home and personal life. Likewise, the character of Yawdy Rum has struggles of his own, particularly managing his declining health. Do you think these challenges are an accurate representation of the challenges that men and women face in today's society? How do they relate to your own personal situation?

2. The character of Yawdy Rum is an unlikely match for Micheal. What is it about Yawdy that allows Micheal to open up and explore a friendship that would otherwise have not lasted beyond their initial meeting on the airplane?

3. Yawdy Rum is teacher, friend, and source of inspiration for Micheal. Who is the Yawdy Rum in your life? In the same sense that Micheal connected with Yawdy, how might we become more open to others around us? How might we benefit from others like Yawdy who have wisdom to share with us in our daily lives?

4. In the end, Yawdy Rum conveys seven basic steps that Micheal can use to harmonize his life. What are some instances in your life where these principles could be effective? Why do you think it's so hard to find the courage to change?

5. Which piece of Yawdy's wisdom did you find most helpful? What, if any, changes are you considering since reading this book?

ABOUT THE AUTHOR

An experienced leader and successful marketing executive, Micheal Lane brings personality, insight, and strategic thinking to his work as an author and professional speaker.

Lane is the founder and president of Mike Lane Productions, through which he provides professional speaking and consulting services. Lane specializes in presentations that educate, motivate, and inspire sales and marketing audiences all across the country.

Lane pulled from his professional and personal experiences to write *The Wisdom of Yawdy Rum*, a story that blends memoir and inspirational writing to help readers learn how to bring lasting positive change to their lives.

Prior to becoming an author and professional speaker, Lane was vice president and director of sales and marketing for Cargill Salt, a division of Cargill, Inc. He has completed over 3,000 hours of specialized training in business management, sales, marketing, and professional speaking. Lane completed his formal writing training at the Loft Literary Center in Minneapolis, in addition to completing the MBA Alternative program through the Carlson School of Management at the University of Minnesota.

Lane resides in Excelsior, Minnesota, with his wife. They have three grown children.

For more information visit
www.LaneSpeaks.com